This book belongs to:

_____

_____

A Treasury
to Read with
Mommy

This edition published by Parragon Books Ltd in 2017 and distributed by

Parragon Inc.
440 Park Avenue South, 13th Floor
New York, NY 10016
www.parragon.com

Cover illustrated by Rebecca Harry

Illustrated by Gabriel Alborozo, Victoria Assanelli, Barroux, Livia Coloji, Abigail Dela Cruz, Marilyn Faucher, Mar Ferrero, Chiara Fiorentino, Henry Fisher, Hannah George, Kim Geyer, Jenny Jones, John Joven, Xuan Le, Emma Levey, Katya Longhi, Mei Matsuoka, Simon Mendez, Davide Ortu, Alessandra Psacharopulo, Gavin Scott, Jaime Temairik, Jenny Wren, and Aleksander Zolotic.

Selected stories retold by Mandy Archer and Claire Sipi.
Original stories written by Catherine Allison, Moira Butterfield,
Deborah Chancellor, Malachy Doyle, and Caroline Pitcher.

Every effort has been made to acknowledge the contributors of this book.
If we have made any errors, we will be pleased to rectify them in future editions.

Designed by Duck Egg Blue and Kate Ford
Edited by Laura Baker and Becky Wilson

ISBN 978-1-4748-7494-6

Printed in China

A Treasury
to Read with
Mommy

PaRragon

Bath · New York · Cologne · Melbourne · Delhi
Hong Kong · Shenzhen · Singapore

Contents

The Fox and the Elephant

Once upon a time, a huge elephant lived in a jungle. The elephant thought he was better than all the other animals because he was so big. He trampled through the jungle, crushing everything on the ground with his big heavy feet, while breaking branches and pushing over small trees with his long trunk. He didn't care that he destroyed the nests of many birds and ruined the underground dens and burrows of the foxes and rabbits.

The other animals were fed up with the elephant and his harmful ways. They called a secret meeting to decide what to do.

"The elephant must be taught a lesson," said a clever fox. "It is the only way to stop him. Leave it to me, and I will come up with a plan."

For several days, the clever fox watched the elephant carefully. Then, after much thinking, he decided on his plan.

The next day, the fox waited for the elephant to start his usual rampage through the jungle. Then, he slipped through the trees and ran ahead, jumping out in front of the elephant.

"Great Sir," said the fox. "I need to speak to you about some urgent business."

The elephant looked down his trunk at the fox. "Who do you think you are to stop me on my morning walk?" he asked rudely.

The clever fox ignored the elephant and said, "Your Highness, all the animals of the jungle have decided to make you our king. I am their messenger and I've come to escort you to the coronation ceremony."

The elephant was very pleased to hear this. He had always wanted to become king of the jungle, so he agreed to follow the fox.

The fox led the elephant to a muddy swamp. Being light of foot, the fox easily crossed it. But when the heavy elephant tried to do the same, he started to sink in the mud. And the more he struggled, the deeper he sank.

"Help me!" he cried.

"Ah, so you see we are important to you!" said the fox. "I will not help you unless you change your mean ways."

The elephant bent his head in shame. "I'm so sorry," he said. "If you help me, I promise I won't cause any more harm."

So the fox dragged a branch over to the elephant, and the elephant climbed out of the swamp. From that day on, he was the kindest of all the animals.

Goldilocks and the Three Bears

Once upon a time there was a little girl named Goldilocks who had beautiful golden hair. She lived in a little cottage right at the edge of the forest.

One morning, before breakfast, Goldilocks skipped into the forest to play. She soon strayed far from home and began to feel hungry.

Just as she was thinking about going home, a delicious smell wafted through the forest. She followed it all the way to a little cottage.

"I wonder who lives here?" thought Goldilocks. She knocked on the door, but there was no answer.

As Goldilocks pushed gently on the door, it swung open and Goldilocks stepped inside.

The delicious smell was coming from three bowls of steaming porridge on a table. There was a great big bowl, a middle-sized bowl, and a teeny-tiny bowl.

Goldilocks was so hungry that she tried the porridge in the biggest bowl first.

"Ooh! Too hot," she cried.

Next she tasted the porridge in the middle-sized bowl.

"Yuck! Too cold," she spluttered.

So Goldilocks tried the porridge in the teeny-tiny bowl.

"Yum," she said. "Just right." And she ate it all up.

Goldilocks saw three comfy chairs by the fire. There was a great big chair, a middle-sized chair, and a teeny-tiny chair.

"Just the place for a nap," yawned Goldilocks sleepily.

She tried to scramble on to the biggest chair. "Too high up!" she gasped, sliding to the ground.

Next Goldilocks tried the middle-sized chair, but she sank into the cushions. "Too squishy!" she grumbled.

So Goldilocks tried the teeny-tiny chair. "Just right!" she sighed, settling down. But Goldilocks was full of porridge and too heavy for the teeny-tiny chair. It squeaked and creaked. Creaked and cracked. Then … CRASH!

It broke into teeny-tiny pieces and Goldilocks fell to the floor.

"Ouch!" she said.

Goldilocks climbed up the stairs. At the top she found a bedroom with three beds. There was a great big bed, a middle-sized bed, and a teeny-tiny bed.

"I'll just lie down for a while," yawned Goldilocks. So she clambered on to the biggest bed. "Too hard," she grumbled.

Then she lay down on the middle-sized bed. "Too soft!" she mumbled.

So she snuggled down in the teeny-tiny bed. "Just right," she sighed, and fell fast asleep.

Meanwhile, a great big daddy bear, a middle-sized mommy bear, and a teeny-tiny baby bear returned home from their walk in the woods.

"The porridge should be cool enough to eat now," said Mommy Bear.

So the three bears went inside their cottage for breakfast.

"Someone's been eating my porridge," growled Daddy Bear, looking in his bowl.

"Someone's been eating my porridge," gasped Mommy Bear, looking in her bowl.

"Someone's been eating my porridge," squeaked Baby Bear, "and they've eaten it all up!"

Then Daddy Bear went over to his chair.

"Someone's been sitting in my chair," he roared. "There's a golden hair on it!"

"Someone's been sitting in my chair," growled Mommy Bear. "The cushions are all squashed."

"Someone's been sitting in my chair," cried Baby Bear, "and they've broken it!"

The three bears stomped upstairs.

Daddy Bear looked at his crumpled bed covers.

"Someone's been sleeping in my bed!" he grumbled.

Mommy Bear looked at the jumbled pillows on her bed.

"Someone's been sleeping in my bed!" she said.

Baby Bear padded over to his bed.

"Someone's been sleeping in my bed," he cried, "and they're still there!"

At that moment, Goldilocks woke up. When she saw the three bears, she leaped out of the bed, ran down the stairs, through the door, into the forest and all the way home! And she never visited the house of the three bears ever again.

The Vain Monk

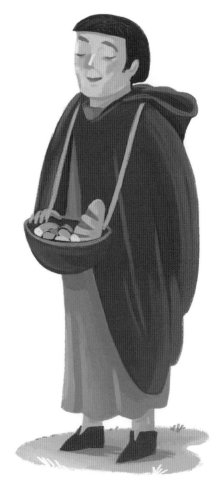

A long time ago, there was a monk who was very proud of himself. He wandered from town to town, seeking money in exchange for his knowledge of holy books. He thought he knew more than everyone he met on his travels.

"These people are lucky that I am coming to ask them for alms," he said when he reached the next town.

As was usual, when the townsfolk saw the monk walking along the street with his wooden bowl, they gave him generous gifts of food and money.

However, the vain monk never bothered to thank them. He thought it was his right because he was so clever.

"I'm so good, everyone can see the greatness in me!" he boasted.

When he got to the edge of the town, he saw a field full of rams. The monk walked into the field toward a huge ram. It lowered its big, sharp horns and began pawing the ground.

"Oh, look!" sighed the monk happily. "Even the animals know how great I am. See how this ram is bowing down to me."

The owner of the rams heard these silly, vain words. He called out to the monk, "Sir! Please be careful. The ram isn't bowing, he's about to attack you!"

"What nonsense!" snapped the monk. "Your ram can see my greatness!"

He had barely finished uttering these ridiculous words, when the ram charged at the monk.

The monk tried to run away, but it was too late. The ram butted him into the air. He fell with a hard bump and dropped his bowl of alms.

"Oh, help me!" he cried. "I think I've broken a bone, and all my food is spoiled!"

"I'm sorry to say it, but you should have listened to me," said the man.

The monk hung his head in shame. "You are right. I'm sorry, I should not have been so vain."

"Well, I think you have learned your lesson now," smiled the man. "Come and have supper at my home."

And from that day on, the monk was never vain again, and he humbly thanked everyone who gave him alms.

Why Owls Stare

Once upon a time there lived an owl and a pigeon. They were friends, but they were great rivals too, and they were always boasting to one another.

"Owls have much better eyesight than pigeons," the owl would claim.

"Pigeons are much better at flying," the pigeon would reply.

"Owls have better hearing," the owl would brag.

"Pigeons have prettier feathers," the pigeon would argue.

One morning they were sitting side by side on a branch when the owl said, "I think there are many more owls than pigeons."

"That can't be right," replied the pigeon. "There are definitely far more pigeons than owls. There's only one way to find out. I challenge you to count them!"

"All right," the owl agreed. "We will need a place with plenty of trees. Let's do it in the Big Woods a week from today. That will give us time to let everyone know."

During that week the owl and the pigeon flew in every direction to tell their fellow birds to come to the Big Woods to be counted.

The day of the count came, and the owls were the first to arrive. It seemed as if every tree was full of owls hooting at each other.

There were so many, the owls were sure they would outnumber the pigeons.

Suddenly the sky went dark. Clouds of pigeons were flying toward the Big Woods. They came from the north, the south, the east, and the west. Soon there was no space left in the trees, and branches were starting to break under the weight of all the pigeons.

More and more pigeons came, circling above the woods, looking for a place to land. By now, the ground was completely covered with pigeons, too. The owls were wide-eyed with amazement as they stared at all the pigeons, who were still arriving by their thousands. The noise of their wings was deafening, and the owls were getting squashed and trampled by the ones who had managed to find a perch in the trees.

"Let's get out of here," the owls hooted to one another, flying away. But the poor creatures had stared so long and hard at the pigeons that their eyes stayed stuck wide open—and from that day on owls always stared, and hid during the day when the pigeons were nearby, flying only at night.

Want to Swap?

It was bedtime, but Duck couldn't sleep. "I'm bored with being a duck and nibbling waterweeds," she said to herself.

Then she saw her friend Rooster strolling around the pond and had a brilliant idea.

"Hey, Rooster," she called. "Want to swap jobs?"

"Okay," Rooster agreed. "Nibbling waterweeds is better than getting up early every day."

So the next morning, Duck waddled to the farmhouse for her first cock-a-doodle-doo to wake up the farmer. But when she opened her beak …

"Quack! Quack! QUACK!"

Poor Duck! However hard she tried, she couldn't crow, and the farmer overslept.

"I want my old job back," Duck said sadly.

Luckily for Duck, Rooster was not enjoying his new job much either.

"Waterweeds are yucky and I kind of miss waking up the farmer," he said.

The next day, when Duck saw Sheepdog herding sheep, she had a thought. She waddled up to the field.

"That looks like fun, Sheepdog," she said. "Want to swap?"

Sheep's Bad Mood

Sheep was in a bad mood. His friends on the farm tried to cheer him up, but their jokes didn't help. Sheep just felt as if there was a growly bear inside him trying to get out.

"I have an idea," said Horse, who was very clever about this sort of thing. "Try doing some hard work."

"How can hard work help?" Sheep grumbled. But no one had any better ideas, so Sheep decided to give it a try. He carried baskets of eggs for the chickens. He lifted bales of hay for the horses. He rode in the tractor with the farmer. He worked so hard that he started to forget about his bad mood. And at bedtime, when all the weary farm animals snuggled down in the barn, Horse noticed that Sheep was smiling.

"Has it gone?" asked Horse.

"Has what gone?" yawned Sheep.

"Your bad mood," said Horse, chuckling loudly.

But there was no reply. Sheep was already fast asleep!

Muddypaws!

It was a special day for Ben. He was so excited. He had a new puppy!

"I'll teach you all the things I know," said Ben. "But first I need to choose a name for you. I'll need to think hard about it. It has to be just perfect."

"I don't really mind what name you choose, as long as you give me lots of cuddles," thought the puppy.

Ben looked around his bedroom to see if he could find an idea for the perfect puppy name.

"I'll look in my storybook," he said, but none of the names in the book were right.

"I think I'll let you hunt for names," thought the new puppy.
"I'd rather look behind that flowerpot."

The little puppy crept over ... He sniffed ... and then he
climbed. He didn't mean to knock the flowerpot over, but ... oops!
That's just what he did. He made muddy paw prints everywhere.

"Let's go to the park. I might be able to think of a good name
there," said Ben.

"I'd rather look behind that tree," thought the little puppy.
So he ran ... and he ran.

He didn't mean to jump in the mud, but ... squelch!

That's just what he did. He made muddy paw prints
everywhere.

Ben's neighbors were having a party in their backyard.

"One of the guests might be able to think of a good name for
you," said Ben. "Let's go and ask them."

"I'd rather look in the pond," thought the new puppy. So he leaned over ... and he leaned over a little bit more. He didn't mean to fall in the pond, but ... splosh! That's just what he did. He made muddy paw prints everywhere.

"We'd better go home and clean you up," said Ben.

"I'd rather go digging in the yard," thought the new puppy.

So he dug … and he dug … and he dug. This time he found lots of things … a lost ring … an old wrench … and a toy car that Ben had lost. He didn't mean to bring all that mud indoors, but … pitter patter … that's just what he did, all over the kitchen floor. He made muddy paw prints everywhere.

And he didn't mean to find a name for himself at last, but … guess what? That's just what he did!

"You are the muddiest, funniest puppy there ever was. There's only one name for you," laughed Ben.

Can you guess what it is?

"Muddypaws!"

How Rabbit Deceived Fox

Long ago, an old widowed woman grew vegetables in her small garden, and sold them to make her living.

The woman worked very hard every day, tending her plants, so she was upset to discover that someone had been stealing some of her cabbages in the night. That someone was the wily Rabbit.

The next night the old woman set a clever trap and caught Rabbit. She tied him up in a sack.

While Rabbit was lying in the sack wondering how he was going to escape, Fox came prowling along. He didn't see the sack on the path in the dark, and he tripped over it.

"What are you doing, hiding in a sack?" asked Fox.

"I'm not hiding," replied Rabbit. "The woman who owns this garden wants me to marry her granddaughter, and when I refused to do it she caught me. She's gone to get the girl now."

"I've been looking for a wife for a long time," said Fox. "I'll marry her. Let me swap places with you."

Fox untied the sack, let Rabbit out and got in it himself. Rabbit tied it back up and hurried away as quickly as he could.

The old woman came back. "I will stop you now, thief!"

When Fox heard these words, he knew Rabbit had tricked him. As soon as the woman opened the sack he sprang out before she could catch him.

Fox was angry at being tricked. He wanted revenge!

Fox found Rabbit sitting on a stone playing his flute.

"What are you doing?" he asked.

"I'm practicing for a wedding," replied Rabbit. "They're going to pay me handsomely. Why don't you join me and share?"

Fox was a greedy fellow, and he thought he'd get the money and then steal the rest from Rabbit.

"I don't have a flute," he said to Rabbit.

"Don't worry, my friend," said the clever Rabbit. "I'll just dash home and get my other flute for you."

Rabbit knew Fox wanted to trick him, so he set fire to the grass around the stone and ran away.

In desperation to save his life, Fox had to jump through the flames. His sleek black coat was scorched to red-brown.

He was so glad to be alive that he decided to forgo his revenge—Rabbit was far too clever for him. But since that night the Rabbit and the Fox have never been friends, and the descendents of this Fox have always had a red-brown coat.

Lion's First Day

It was clumsy Lion's first day at Miss Giraffe's Savannah School. True to his nature, he arrived late, skidded into the classroom, tripped over his paws, and landed upside down in his chair.

Miss Giraffe tilted her head and smiled kindly at Lion.

"What an amazing acrobat you are!" she said.

At lunchtime, Lion bumped into the table and knocked all the food over. Then he spilled his drink and slipped across the floor.

"What wonderful clown skills you have!" said Miss Giraffe.

At playtime, Lion tripped over and knocked some balls off a shelf, catching three with his paws and one on the tip of his tail.

"What a fantastic juggler you'd make!" said Miss Giraffe.

That evening, Lion couldn't wait to tell his mother about his day.

"All this time I thought I was clumsy, but Miss Giraffe thinks I'm an acrobat!" he said. "And a clown and a juggler!"

His mother smiled.

"You can be a magician too—just make your dinner disappear!"

Fluff's Muddle

Fluff the owl was all in a muddle. During the daytime, when owls should be asleep, Fluff was wide awake. There was just so much happening on the farm! She giggled at the geese waddling around the pond and chuckled as the chickens scratched and pecked the ground. She laughed so much that she kept waking up her family.

"You're too noisy," said her sister, Blink.

"You're keeping us awake!" said her brother, Beak.

That night, Fluff was feeling tired, just when owls should be wide awake.

"I know what we can do to fix Fluff's muddle," said Blink.

Fluff could hardly believe her eyes as Blink and Beak waddled round the pond like geese, and scratched and pecked the ground like chickens. She laughed so much that it kept her awake all night.

By the time morning came, Fluff was feeling very tired indeed. The geese waddled and the chickens scratched and pecked as usual, but Fluff was fast asleep.

The Sad Princess

A long time ago, there lived a sad princess. She had a beautiful home and a loving family, but she never laughed. The king and queen didn't know what to do. They just wanted their daughter to be happy. So one day, the king declared, "Whoever makes my daughter laugh can marry her!"

Young men from all over the kingdom came to try to make the sad princess chuckle. But even their funniest jokes didn't make her smile.

Several months passed and still the princess did not laugh. The king, who had almost given up hope, went to see his daughter in her room. A strange noise greeted him. The princess was standing by the window, roaring with laughter. The king rushed over to the window to see what was making her giggle.

On the road outside the palace, a man was trying to get his donkey to move, but the stubborn creature was refusing. The man was pulling so hard on the rope that he kept falling over. And the more the man toppled over, the more the princess chuckled.

"Young man, you may marry my daughter!" the king called out.

And so the princess was married and lived a happy life, full of laughter.

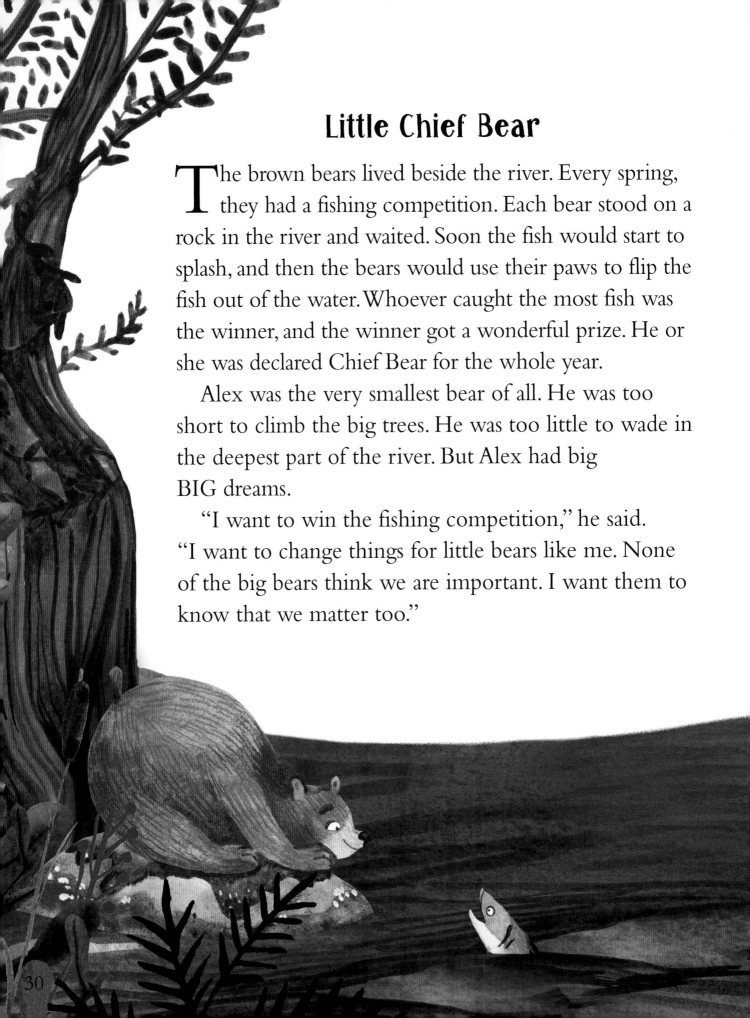

Little Chief Bear

The brown bears lived beside the river. Every spring, they had a fishing competition. Each bear stood on a rock in the river and waited. Soon the fish would start to splash, and then the bears would use their paws to flip the fish out of the water. Whoever caught the most fish was the winner, and the winner got a wonderful prize. He or she was declared Chief Bear for the whole year.

Alex was the very smallest bear of all. He was too short to climb the big trees. He was too little to wade in the deepest part of the river. But Alex had big BIG dreams.

"I want to win the fishing competition," he said. "I want to change things for little bears like me. None of the big bears think we are important. I want them to know that we matter too."

Everyone laughed when Alex joined the competition. "You're too little to be a good fisher," said one of the bigger bears. "You're too little to be good at anything!"

Even the Chief Bear laughed at him. "Leave the fishing to the big bears," he said. "Go and play with the other babies."

But Alex put his chin up and stepped on to a rock in the middle of the river. The other bears laughed again.

"He'll never win," they said, shaking their heads. "He should just give up."

Alex didn't say anything. He just peered into the water, looking for fish. There was a silvery flash and he splashed his paw into the water.

"Missed," said one of the biggest bears, chuckling. "You had better give up."

Alex put his head down and looked into the water again. This time he didn't try to catch the fish. He just watched. And after a few minutes, he noticed something. The fish were clever! They could see the bears, and they were trying to swim away from danger. But they didn't realize that Alex was a bear too—they were swimming straight toward him.

Flick! One fish landed on the rock beside Alex. Flick! Flick! His paw moved so fast that the fish didn't see him coming. His pile of fish grew larger and larger and larger. The minutes went by, and at last the Chief Bear held up his paw.

"Stop!" he said. "The competition is over. Now it's time to count the fish."

When all the fish had been counted, the Chief Bear's mouth fell open in surprise. Then he climbed on to a log and looked around at all the bears.

"We have all been very silly," he said. "We thought that because Alex was small, he wasn't as good as us. But Alex is better than us. He has won the competition! Alex is our new Chief Bear."

He stepped down from the log, and Alex stepped up to take his place. He couldn't see very well, so he stood up on his hind legs.

"I will try to be a good Chief," he said. "And my first command is that all bears, big and small, must be treated equally, because they are just as important as each other!"

The Monkey and the Foolish Tigers

Lion, the king of the jungle, had invited all the animals to a big feast to celebrate the birth of his son. There was much noise and laughter as the happy animals danced the night away and ate the delicious food.

By morning, the tables were covered in crumbs. As the animals helped to clear up, two tigers spotted a large slice of cake. It was on a plate under a shady tree.

"Ooh, yummy!" purred one of the tigers. "No one seems to have noticed it. I'm going to eat it for my breakfast."

The other tiger looked at his friend. "You can't. It's mine. I saw it first!"

"Keep away from it!" shouted the first tiger. "It was my idea to have it for breakfast."

And so the two tigers carried on arguing.

A monkey had been watching the tigers with amusement. He couldn't believe how foolish they were.

"Gentlemen! Don't fight," he cried in a loud voice. "Let me share the cake between the two of you."

Reluctantly, as they couldn't agree upon a solution themselves, the tigers pushed the plate toward the monkey.

The cheeky monkey split the cake into two pieces.

"Oh no!" he sighed. "This won't do. One piece is bigger than the other."

So he took a bite out of the larger slice.

"Oh, silly me!" said the monkey. "Now this piece is smaller than the other one."

Then he took another bite from the second slice. Each time, one of the pieces remained bigger than the other … and the monkey kept eating until, finally, the whole slice of cake was gone.

"Oh, dear," laughed the monkey. "There's none left!" And, quick as a flash, he jumped up into the tree and scampered away.

The foolish tigers realized they had been tricked by the clever monkey.

"If only we hadn't argued," groaned the first tiger. "Then we both could have had some of that cake!"

Merry's Big Wish

Once upon a time there was a beautiful wooden horse named Merry who lived on a merry-go-round on the end of a boardwalk by the beach. But Merry wasn't just an ordinary wooden horse. He was very special! Every day people would come along to pat his nose and make a wish. And almost always that wish would come true. For you see, Merry was said to have come from a magical land far away.

Merry loved giving rides to all the little children, and he loved making wishes come true. But Merry had a wish of his own.

He wished he were real, so that he could gallop across the soft sand and splash through gentle waves on the seashore.

One night, when everyone had gone home for the day, Merry heard a neigh and a beautiful white mare appeared.

"Come with me," called the mare.

"I can't," replied Merry. "I'm not real."

"Anything is possible," said the mare, blowing softly on Merry's well-rubbed nose. Suddenly a strange feeling came over Merry. His nose began to tingle and his legs began to twitch. Then he kicked his legs into the air and he was free. He raced after the white mare and splashed through the waves.

"Neigghhh!" cried Merry, as he and the white mare galloped on and on through the night. They didn't stop until they came to a faraway land full of snowy white horses.

"Where are we?" asked Merry.

"This is your home," replied the white mare. "The land where you came from. From now on you will live here with us."

"But what about the merry-go-round and all the little children? And what about the wishes?"

"Don't worry," replied the white mare. "You can work on the merry-go-round each day, then return home each night."

"Neigghhh!" squealed Merry, tossing his mane into the air. "Now I am the happiest horse in the world."

Sammy's Tree

Sammy the monkey sat in the biggest fruit tree in the jungle and bossed his friends around.

"No other monkeys allowed today," he would say. "Don't eat those berries. Don't sit there."

"Sammy always saves the best fruit for himself," his friends complained. "It's not fair." One by one, they stopped coming to the tree.

Eventually, no monkeys came at all.

"Where is everyone?" Sammy asked.

"They don't like being bossed around," squawked a parrot.

Sammy felt sad. He had driven his friends away.

"Please tell everyone that they can eat as much as they like," he said. "I just want my friends back."

Next day, the tree was full of monkeys! Sammy didn't boss anyone around. He just laughed and played with his friends.

"Being in charge of the tree was fun," he said. "But playing with my friends is even better!"

Hide and Seek

James the meerkat played with his friend Bernard in the zoo every day. But this morning, Bernard was nowhere to be found.

"Maybe he's hiding," said James, standing on his back legs and looking all around. "I'll search the zoo."

James wriggled through the fence and scampered to the elephant house. "Have you seen Bernard?" he asked. The elephants shook their heads.

James went to see the crocodiles. "Have you seen Bernard?" he asked. They just snapped their jaws.

None of the other zoo animals had seen Bernard. James walked sadly back home and wriggled through the fence.

"SURPRISE!" shouted a friendly voice. It was Bernard, holding up a birthday cake! A big smile spread over James's face.

"I forgot it was my birthday," he said, blowing out the candles. "But I already have my birthday wish. My best friend is back!"

The Fox and the Stork

Once upon a time, a fox decided to play a trick on his neighbor, the stork.

"Would you like to come and have supper with me?" he asked her one morning.

The stork was surprised by the invitation, because the fox had never been friendly to her before, but she happily accepted. He looked like a well-fed beast, and she was sure he would provide her with a good meal.

Every now and then, through the day, the stork caught the mouth-watering smell of the soup that the fox was preparing. By the time she arrived at his home, she was feeling very hungry—which was exactly what the fox wanted.

"Enjoy your meal," said the crafty fox, ladling the soup into a shallow bowl. Of course, the fox was able to lap his up easily, but the stork could only dip the tip of her bill into the soup. She wasn't able to drink a single drop!

"Mmm, that was delicious," said the fox when he had slurped up the soup. "I see you don't have much of an appetite, so I will have yours, too."

The poor stork went home feeling hungrier than ever and was determined to take her revenge on the sly fox for playing such a mean trick. So, the following week, she went to see him.

"Thank you for inviting me to supper last week," she said. "Now I would like to return the favor. Please come and dine with me this evening."

The fox was a little suspicious that the stork might want to pay him back, but he didn't see how she could possibly play a trick on him. After all, he was known for his cunning, and very few creatures had ever managed to outwit him.

All day long the fox looked forward to his supper, and by the evening he was very hungry. As he approached the stork's home he caught the appetizing aroma of a fish stew and started to lick his lips.

But when the stork served the stew it was in a tall pot with a very narrow neck. The stork could reach the food easily with her long bill, but the fox could only lick the rim of the pot and sniff the tempting smell. As much as he didn't want to, the fox had to admit he had been outsmarted—and he went home with an empty stomach!

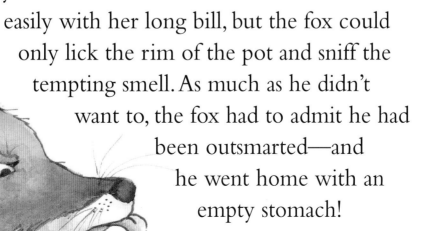

That's Not My Brother!

The ducklings were off for their very first swim.
Dora cried, "I want to join in!"
"Come on!" called her brother. "You're always late!"
And he followed the other ducks under the gate.
"Where's my brother?" cried Dora.

"Lost your brother?" asked Frog. "I heard a few quacks.
And look! I am sure those are brother-duck tracks!"
So off Dora waddled, with Frog beside her,
Till they came to a spot where the path was wider.
"He's here!" Dora cried as she looked up and saw
That the tracks led right up to a big nest of straw.
"That's not my brother!" she cried. "It's Hen!"

"Lost your brother?" smiled Hen, with a chirpy cluck-cluck.
"Those tracks in the straw might just bring you more luck!"
"It's this way!" cried Frog. "Come along, little buddy!"
"Are you sure?" questioned Dora. "It looks kind of muddy."
They heard something squelching behind a big tree,
And Frog said, "That sounds like your brother to me!"
"That's not my brother!" cried Dora. "It's Pig!"

"Lost your brother?" said Pig, in his cool, muddy hollow.
"Look, there are other fresh tracks you can follow!"
The grass was so tall that they kept tripping over
As they followed the tracks through a big field of clover.
"I don't think that these tracks are a duckling's, do you?"
Said Dora, as a very loud voice went ... "MOO!"
"That's not my brother!" cried Dora. "It's Cow!"

"Lost your brother?" said Cow, as she chewed on her dinner.
"Try those little tracks, where the grass is much thinner."
Dora took Frog on a piggyback ride …
All the way to the barn, where the tracks led inside.
"Found him!" cried Frog. "He just dashed through the door …
To nibble a few grains of wheat off the floor!"
"That's not my brother!" cried Dora. "It's Mouse!"

"Lost your brother?" squeaked Mouse. "These tracks are ours.
But who made those prints over there by the flowers?"
"He's here in the garden, right under our noses!"
Said Frog as they followed the tracks through the roses.
And then the tracks stopped. Frog declared, "Look, his feet!
Your brother is hiding behind that pink sheet!"
"That's not my brother!"cried Dora. "It's Goat!"

"Lost your brother?" said Goat, his mouth full of sweater.
"If you follow those tracks to the trough you'll do better."
Frog hopped ahead, then he gave a great shout.
"Hey, listen!" he cried. "Who's that splashing about?"
Dora quacked happily, "That must be him!
He's in the old water trough, having a swim."
"That's not my brother!" cried Dora. "It's Puppy!"

"Lost your brother?" yapped Puppy. "No need to despair!
I think you should look by the pond over there."
When they got to the pond there were no ducks in sight.
"But look at these prints," Dora said. "Puppy's right!
They're definitely duck tracks, and so are these others,
Which means," Dora grinned, "that I've found …
… all my brothers!"

The Cunning Hare and the Lion

There was once a powerful lion who ruled the jungle. He was cruel and killed the other animals whenever he felt like it. The animals had had enough, so they went to the lion's den.

"Oh, Master, you kill many of us every day without necessity," they cried. "One animal a day is enough to satisfy your hunger. Please come to an agreement with us. Starting from today, we promise to offer one among us to you every day. In this way, you will not have to hunt and many of our lives will be spared."

The lion thought about this for a moment. "Okay, I agree, but if I do not receive an animal every day, I will kill all of you!"

With the agreement in place, the animals happily went about their business, and only one unlucky creature was sent to the lion each day.

One day a hare was chosen. He didn't want to become the lion's dinner, so he came up with a clever plan.

"You have made me wait all day for my dinner!" roared the hungry lion, when the hare eventually arrived at the den. "I will eat you and then kill all the other animals."

"Oh, Master, don't do that," pleaded the hare. "I can explain. On the way here I met another lion who said he was the king of the jungle, and that we should only offer ourselves as food to him. He says you are an imposter."

On hearing this, the lion was furious. "Take me to this pretender. I will show him who's king of the jungle!"

The hare led the lion to a well.

"Sire, the lion lives in that den down there," said the hare. The lion looked into the well and saw his own reflection, which he thought was the other lion. With a mighty roar he leaped into the well—and that was the end of him!

The hare was given a hero's celebration for his cleverness. And from then on, the animals lived happily in peace in the jungle.

The Birds, the Beasts, and the Bat

A long time ago, the birds and the beasts had many disagreements. They decided to have a battle to settle their differences once and for all.

Poor Bat, who had wings like the birds and fur like the beasts, didn't know what to do. He didn't want to fight, but he didn't want to be caught on the losing side, either.

So when the birds asked him who he supported, he quickly replied, "I have wings! I am on your side, of course."

And when the beasts asked him which side he would join, he responded, "Isn't it obvious? I have fur and sharp teeth. I'm with you!"

Luckily, at the last minute, the birds and the beasts made peace and no battle was fought.

With a huge sigh of relief, Bat went to join in the celebrations. But when the birds and the beasts realized that Bat had been on both sides, they turned on him angrily.

Now poor Bat lives in fear, hiding in dark places and only flying out at night.

The Owl and the Grasshopper

In a dark forest, there lived an owl. She had become very grumpy in her old age and didn't like being woken up from her daily nap.

One afternoon, as Owl dozed in her hollow, a grasshopper began his raspy song.

Owl woke with a start. Poking her head out of the tree, she hooted, "Have you no manners? Go away and leave me in peace to sleep!"

"You can't tell me what to do!" replied the bold grasshopper. And he struck up a louder, scratchier tune.

Owl realized she couldn't make the grasshopper stop. She also knew that she couldn't see him very well in the day to catch him. So she called out in a sweet voice, "If I must stay awake, come and sing closer to me in my cozy tree."

Flattered, the foolish grasshopper jumped into Owl's dark hollow. Owl tried to stop him singing by eating him up! Luckily the grasshopper escaped, but from that day on, he always thought of others before he sang.

Surprise Out Shopping

When Benjamin Mouse saw a blue bike in the toy store window, Mr. Mouse said bikes were silly. Benjamin thought his daddy was a bit too serious.

"Help me do the shopping instead," Mr. Mouse said.

"Shopping is boring," grumbled Benjamin.

"Perhaps it'll be more fun than you think," said Mr. Mouse.

At the grocer's, Mr. Mouse picked out some carrots and some apples. Out of the corner of his eye, Benjamin saw the grocer juggle some apples and oranges. He told his daddy, who frowned.

"Grocers are too sensible to juggle," he said.

At the dairy, while Mr. Mouse collected some milk and cheese, Benjamin saw Mrs. Cow twirling in a pink tutu. He told his daddy, who shook his head.

"Cows are far too busy to dance," he said.

The final stop was the bakery. While Mr. Mouse was busy choosing some tasty rolls and buns, Benjamin saw the baker balancing fifteen doughnuts on the tip of her nose. Benjamin told his daddy, who sighed.

"You're imagining things," he said. "Bakers don't play with their food."

As they passed the toy store on the way home, the door opened and the toymaker wheeled out the blue bike.

"Oh, no," gasped Benjamin. "It's been sold!"

"Yes, it has," said the toymaker. "It belongs to YOU!"

Benjamin stared at his daddy in amazement.

"Did you buy it?" he asked.

"Me?" Mr. Mouse said. "I'm far too serious to buy toys!"

But he exchanged a secret wink with the toymaker as Benjamin jumped on to the bike in excitement.

"I'll help with the shopping again tomorrow," Benjamin promised. "You were right—it's much more fun than I thought!"

Daisy's Big Adventure

Once upon a time there was a marmalade kitten called Daisy who belonged to a little boy named Charlie. Daisy was a very happy little kitten. When she wasn't having fun in the yard, she spent her days playing in Charlie's bedroom. She loved playing with Charlie's toys and knew every one of them by name. And after a hard day's playing, Daisy would curl up and go to sleep on Charlie's bed.

One morning Daisy awoke to find something new sitting on Charlie's bedroom floor. It was a big, square, wooden thing.

"What can it be?" wondered Daisy. She sniffed the "thing" gingerly and prodded it with her paw. "Maybe it's a new place for me to sleep," she thought. And she leaped inside to try it out. But she leaped out again immediately. The "thing" was full of tiny people. They were dressed in fine clothes and looked very important. One of them was even riding a horse!

"Who are they and where have they come from?" she wondered. She hid behind the jack-in-the-box and watched to see what they would do. Daisy waited and waited, but the tiny people did not move. Even the horse stayed perfectly still.

"How strange," thought Daisy. She crept out from her hiding place and gave one of the people a nudge. The poor fellow fell to the ground and didn't move.

"I am sorry," she meowed. "I hope I haven't hurt you."

Just then, Charlie woke up. When he heard Daisy meowing he jumped out of bed and picked her up.

"What are you doing?" he laughed, giving her a hug. "Are you playing with my new castle and toy soldiers?"

"Ahhh," thought Daisy. "So that's why they don't move. They're toys!"

From that day on, the castle became Daisy's favorite toy. She liked nothing better than playing soldiers and kittens. But the game she enjoyed best was knights and dragons—with Daisy as the dragon, of course.

The Smiling Fish

Mateo the fish lived deep, deep under the sea. His home was so far down that there was hardly any light at all. Everything around Mateo was gloomy and dark. In fact, the only thing that wasn't dull was Mateo! He was as bright as the sun, and his smile was even brighter. But Mateo had never seen the sun. He had never seen the sky or felt the wind on his face.

"What is it like up there?" Mateo asked his friend the crab.

The crab tapped his claws on a rock.

"It's very hot and bright," he said. "And it's dangerous, because there are humans up there. They are all cruel. They want to catch fish and crabs and eat them up."

The other deep-sea creatures gathered around too.

"He's right," said the jellyfish. "Humans are not our friends."

"I was caught in a net once," said the swordfish with a shiver. "I had to cut my way out."

"It sounds amazing up there," said Mateo. "I want to see the beautiful sun and watch the waves. I even want to see some humans. They can't all be bad."

The other creatures shook their heads and stared at Mateo.

"Going to the surface is too risky," said the crab.

But Mateo thought about the sunshine and the waves and the breeze, and he couldn't stay down in the deep sea any longer. He swam up, up, UP!

The water began to get lighter. Everything started to look a little less gloomy. Then it looked a LOT less gloomy. And then, at last, his head broke through the water and he felt the cool wind on his scales. A huge smile spread across his face. His colorful scales sparkled in the sunshine, and his smile was dazzling. It was even spotted by a family fishing from a boat.

"What a beautiful fish!" said the little girl. "He's awesome!"

"Let's catch him," said the girl's brother, and their father agreed. The boy cast his line into the water. It bobbed toward Mateo.

Mateo gazed at the fishing line. He had never seen one before, and he didn't know what it was. He swam a little closer.

"Swim away!" the girl shouted to Mateo. "Stay free!"

Mateo plunged down into the water, away from the fishing line. The boy and his father groaned, but the girl smiled. When Mateo was at a safe distance, he turned and smiled too. He knew that he had made a human friend. Then he turned and dived down, down, down to his gloomy home.

Everything seemed different now that he had seen the surface. His friends were waiting for him. When they saw him come back safely, they cheered and danced around.

"How did you stay safe?" asked the crab.

"It was all thanks to a human girl," said Mateo. "Not all humans want to catch fish. Some people just want to be friends!"

The Three Little Pigs

Once upon a time, three little pigs lived together with their mother. One day it was time for them to leave home and build houses of their own.

"Be careful of the big, bad wolf," warned their mother as they trotted off down the road.

The first little pig built his house from straw.

Before long the big, bad wolf came to call.

"Little pig, little pig, let me come in," growled the wolf, licking his lips. He had come for his supper.

"Not by the hairs on my chinny-chin-chin!" the first little pig replied.

"Well, I'll huff and I'll puff and I'll blow your house down!" snarled the wolf. And that's just what he did. The little pig ran away as fast as he could.

The second little pig decided to build his house from sticks.

When the wolf saw the house, he pushed his nose against the door, and growled, "Little pig, little pig, let me come in."

"Not by the hairs on my chinny-chin-chin!" cried the second little pig.

"Well, I'll huff and I'll puff and I'll blow your house down!" snarled the wolf. And that's just what he did. The little pig ran away as fast as he could.

The third little pig built a strong house from bricks. He had just put a pot of soup on the fire to boil when he saw his brothers running down the path, closely followed by the wolf.

"Quick!" cried the third little pig. He opened the door and let his brothers inside.

"Little pigs, little pigs, let me come in!" roared the wolf.

"Not by the hairs on our chinny-chin-chins," cried the three little pigs.

"Well, I'll huff and I'll puff and I'll blow your house down!" snarled the wolf. So he huffed and he puffed … and he huffed and he puffed … but the house stood firm.

The wolf climbed on to the roof and slid down the chimney—straight into the pot of hot soup.

"Owwwoooo!" he cried.

The wolf leaped up and ran out of the house, never to be seen again!

The Brave Little Tailor

One day, the little tailor was eating some toast with honey when he noticed some flies buzzing around him. He grabbed a scrap of material off his workbench and swatted them all at once.

"Wow! Seven flies in one blow," he cried happily. He was so pleased with himself that he stitched the words "seven in one blow" on to his belt.

The tailor decided to go on a little adventure to show off his bravery. He put on his belt, then grabbed a loaf of bread and some cheese.

Outside, he saw a bird pecking in the dirt.

"Come with me on my adventure, little bird," the tailor cried, "and you can eat as much bread as you please."

The tailor carefully put the bird in his pocket, then set off down the road toward the mountains. Before long, he met a giant who had been scaring the villagers for years.

Feeling brave, the tailor shouted out, "Good day, dear fellow!"

"How dare you talk to me!" roared the giant. Just then, the giant read the words on the tailor's belt. He thought the tailor had killed seven giants with one blow!

The giant didn't believe this, so he picked up a rock and squeezed it into little pieces. "Bet you can't do that, little man!"

"No problem," laughed the tailor, and he took the lump of cheese from his bag and squeezed it into tiny pieces.

The giant picked up another rock and threw it into the sky. "Bet you can't throw as high as that!"

The tailor gently lifted the bird out of his pocket and threw it up into the air. The bird flew even higher into the sky.

The giant couldn't believe his eyes. "Well, if you're such a strong, brave fellow, come and spend the night in my cave."

The tailor followed the giant to his cave. The bed was too big for the tailor, so when the giant fell asleep, the tailor crawled into a dark corner of the cave.

That night, the giant hurled a huge branch on to the bed. CRASH! Thinking he'd killed the tailor, the giant ran into the village.

When the villagers saw the giant, they screamed in fear. Suddenly, out of the dark, the little tailor appeared.

"This mighty giant couldn't destroy me!" he shouted.

The giant thought he was seeing a ghost and was terrified. He ran away as fast as he could, never to be seen again.

Everyone in the village was very grateful to the little tailor for his bravery.

Billy's First Day

Billy loved to do new things, but he couldn't think of anything new to do today. "I've tried swinging upside down," he said to Mom. "I've made mud pies, ridden a unicycle, learned magic tricks, and walked on stilts. What next?"

"Have you forgotten?" asked Mom. "You're starting school today."

"What if there's nothing new to do?" Billy worried.

"You might be surprised," his mom said.

Billy's teacher was called Mr. Lemon. "Today you'll learn to write your own name on all your books," he said. "Then you'll try rope climbing, then I'll teach you to play a song on the piano."

It was an amazing day. Billy learned five new games, made six friends, and even made a magic potion that bubbled all over the classroom!

"How was your first day?" Mom asked at home time.

"AWESOME!" Billy replied, grinning. "I'll never run out of new things to do in school!"

Poor George

Absolutely nothing about George's life was normal. You see, George's mom was a witch and his dad was a wizard. George's clothes weren't washed in a machine—they were washed by magic! But whenever George tried the spell, it went a bit wrong. That's how his gym suit turned pink with brown splodges. Poor George!

George's dinner wasn't cooked in the oven—it was cooked by magic. But when George cooked dinner, the spells got mixed up. That's why he had blue burgers and red yogurt to eat. Poor George!

One evening, George had a brainwave. He could do his homework by magic!

"Abracadabra!" BANG! One of the books turned into a purple frog. George tried again.

PUFF! Another book became a green parrot. George sighed, dropped the wand and picked up a pen.

"Maybe I'll do my homework the normal way," he said. Poor George!

Just One More Swim

Big Bear stood up and sniffed the air, then lumbered out toward the water. Her cubs scampered after her, blinking at the dazzling world.

Big Bear padded across the ice. She stopped and dug a hole. She dipped in her paw and scooped out a fish!

The cubs did just what Big Bear did. One dug a hole. The other pounced on the cloud of white, and frightened off the fish. The cubs squabbled. They fought. They tackled each other and tumbled and rolled, over and over in the snow.

They ran and raced on their snowshoe paws, and tummy-tobogganed on the ice. But then they stopped and stared.

"What is that?" they asked, gazing at the blue-green water.

Every morning, Big Bear coaxed her cubs a little farther toward the ocean. Then one day, Big Bear and her cubs slowly and carefully made their way to the water's edge. Big Bear gently slid into the icy sea.

"Come back!" squealed the cubs. But Big Bear swam out strongly to an island of ice in the waves.

The cubs waited, shivering on the thin ice. The water rippled. The cubs patted it—but it just wouldn't stay still. Then they put two paws in … and pulled them right back out again.

Big Bear called to her cubs to swim over to the island. "Come to me across the ocean," she urged. "You can do it! Swim!"

And the cubs did! Under the water they went, twisting and turning in the aquamarine sea. Then they dived down from on high, cutting through the waves, paddling with their paws. They splashed and somersaulted through the icy water. They paddled and swam until Big Bear insisted, "Come out now!"

The cubs pulled their weary bodies on to the ice. Then Big Bear led her cubs to where the juicy blueberries grew. The cubs ate and ate, until their muzzles and paws turned blue.

Big Bear sprawled on her back, enjoying the sunshine on her damp fur. But the cubs had other ideas. And, as they headed back toward the water one more time, Big Bear smiled as she heard their call …

"Just one more swim!"

The Nose that Knows

Milo loves his owner.
She's a girl called Molly Brown.
But Milo's nose loves food the most …
It leads him all round town.

For Milo's nose is a nose that knows—
It knows when food is near.
When it smells a smell, the nose soon shows
Poor Milo where to steer!

Molly's heading out with Mom.
Milo follows. BARK! BARK!
But the nose has sniffed a SANDWICH
Moving quickly through the park.

Where the nose goes, Milo goes …
SPLASH! So now he's paddling through a pond!
Then his nose smells APPLES
Of which he's really rather fond …!

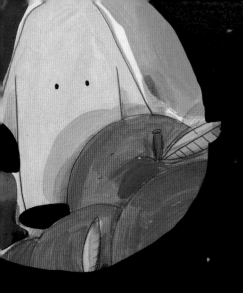

They're in a massive rocket—
He'll just grab one and then he'll go.
He sneaks in, but the doors close ...
SIX

FIVE

FOUR

THREE

TWO

ONE ...

WHOA!

Milo's now in outer space,
Whoosh, zoom, putter, splutter.

Out he climbs and finds the moon
Is made of PEANUT BUTTER!

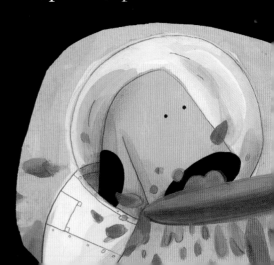

Then his nose smells something else oh so nice.
It's miles away, but it smells just like paradise.
His nose, it knows what's cooking—it's his favorite thing to eat …
Cooking on a barbecue, it's yummy, sizzling MEAT!

"Hey, you're back!" cries Molly. "Wherever did you go?"
Milo wags his tail, but she will never know!
Molly's just glad he's home and gives him ONE HUGE TREAT.
Milo's glad to be back too, and glad—at last—to eat.

So Milo, he might wander. Yes Milo, he might roam.
But Milo's nose is a nose that knows and always leads him …

HOME!

Billy Fox Is Bored

Billy looked out of the kitchen window and sighed. It was so cold and windy that he couldn't go out to play.

He had played with all of his toys. He had finished his favorite book. He had tidied up his bedroom, and had even straightened out his sock drawer. Now there was nothing left to do but peer out of the window and watch the leaves blow by.

"I'm bored," he sighed. "There's nothing to do. Can't I go outside?"

"No," replied Dad gently. "There's a big storm on its way and I don't want you to get caught in it. Why don't we just spend a little time together?"

"But staying inside is boring," moaned Billy Fox. "I want to go out and play with my friends."

"I'm afraid you can't," Dad said firmly. "Do you want to help me make cakes instead? They're your favorite—Woodland Crunch."

"I suppose so," muttered Billy, not sounding at all interested. He watched his dad pour the ingredients into a bowl and sighed wearily.

"Come on," smiled Dad. "Help me mix it all together." He passed Billy a wooden spoon and soon they were both stirring the bowl energetically.

"Brrrrrrr!" went Dad, pretending to be a cement mixer.

"Brrrrrrr!" Billy joined in. And soon Billy actually found that, much to his surprise, he was enjoying himself.

Before long, the cakes were ready to go into the hot oven.

"Now we just have to wait for them to cook," said Dad.

"But that's ages!" said Billy.

"Sit back and I'll tell you a story while we wait," suggested Dad. "Once upon a time …"

Dad finished the story just as the cakes came out of the oven. Before long Billy was munching one.

"That was good," cried Billy, licking his lips. "But not as good as spending time with you, Dad. Can we do it again tomorrow?"

Chicken Licken

One day, an acorn fell on Chicken Licken's head, then rolled away.

"Oh, my," clucked Chicken Licken, panicked. "THE SKY IS FALLING!"

"Cluck-a-cluck-cluck!" shrieked Henny Penny. "We must tell the king!"

So they flapped down the road, and met Cocky Locky.

"Where are you going in such a hurry?" he asked.

"THE SKY IS FALLING!" cried Chicken Licken. "We're off to tell the king!"

"Cock-a-doodle-doo," crowed Cocky Locky. "I'll come, too!"

So Chicken Licken, Henny Penny, and Cocky Locky rushed off to tell the king. Soon they met Ducky Lucky.

"Why are you flapping so?" she asked.

"THE SKY IS FALLING!" cried Chicken Licken. "We're off to tell the king!"

"C-can I c-c-come?" quacked Ducky Lucky nervously.

So Chicken Licken, Henny Penny, Cocky Locky, and Ducky Lucky rushed off to tell the king.

Soon they met Drakey Lakey.

"What's all this fuss?" he asked.

"THE SKY IS FALLING!" cried Chicken Licken. "We're off to tell the king!"

"I'll join you," squawked Drakey Lakey.

So Chicken Licken, Henny Penny, Cocky Locky, Ducky Lucky, and Drakey Lakey rushed off to tell the king.

Soon they met Goosey Loosey and Turkey Lurkey.

"What's ruffled your feathers?" Goosey Loosey asked.

"THE SKY IS FALLING!" cried Chicken Licken. "We're off to tell the king!"

"Goodness," gobbled Turkey Lurkey.

"We'll come!" honked Goosey Loosey.

So Chicken Licken, Henny Penny, Cocky Locky, Ducky Lucky, Drakey Lakey, Goosey Loosey, and Turkey Lurkey rushed off to tell the king.

Soon they met Foxy Loxy.

"Hello!" he said. "Where are you all going?"

"THE SKY IS FALLING!" cried Chicken Licken. "We're off to tell the king!"

Foxy Loxy grinned slyly. "I know a short cut. Follow me."

So they did … right into Foxy Loxy's den!

"RUN!" cried Chicken Licken.

And the seven birds ran home, flapping and flurrying, as fast as they could.

And they never did get to tell the king about the sky falling.

The Little Brother and the Little Sister

A long time ago, a little brother and his little sister lived with their stepmother on the edge of a forest. The stepmother was very cruel to them.

One night, the little brother and the little sister ran away.

The children crept into the forest and wandered past many trees until they came to a clearing by a stream.

"Let's sleep here tonight," said the little brother. "We can decide where to go tomorrow."

They curled up in the hollow of a tree, near the water's edge.

But their stepmother was actually a wicked witch. When she realized that the children were missing, she put a curse on all the streams in the forest.

The children woke up very thirsty. They walked over to the stream to drink from it.

Suddenly, a whispery voice called out from the water.

"Beware! This water has been cursed. Don't drink from me or you will become a deer!"

The little sister reached out to stop her brother, but it was too late! He had already taken a sip. Her brother was turned into a deer.

The little sister was afraid, but she soon found her courage.

"Don't worry," she told her brother. "We'll live in the forest. I'll look after you."

For many years, they lived happily.

Then, one day, a passing hunter shot the deer's leg with an arrow. The deer managed to limp home to his sister. The hunter, who happened to be a prince, followed the deer. When he saw the sister tenderly nursing the wounded deer, he fell in love with her.

The sister married the prince, and she took the deer to the palace to live with them.

Many happy years passed, and the sister and her deer brother had almost forgotten about their cruel stepmother.

Then, one day, the wicked witch found out where they lived. She crept into the palace to cast another evil curse over them … But the prince's guard dogs chased her away and in the commotion the witch's spell was cast on herself! She vanished into thin air.

With the witch gone, the brother's curse was broken. He returned to his human self, and the brother and the sister lived at the palace for many happy years.

The Pirate King

The Pirate King was in trouble. Another pirate had attacked his ship. A fierce battle had taken place. Even though they were outnumbered, the Pirate King had fought bravely, but in the end, all his men had deserted him and had left on the other pirate ship.

"How can I rule the ocean waves all by myself?" he sniffed, sailing toward a little desert island. "I'll stay here. I have nothing else to do."

But no pirate stays gloomy for long. "I belong on the ocean waves!" he cried. "I'll be the crew and the captain!" He jumped back on board his ship, pulled on his pirate hat, and set sail, with the Jolly Roger waving in the breeze, to look for treasure and adventure.

A few days later, the Pirate King spotted another ship. He aimed all his cannons at it and ... BOOM! BOOM!

"We surrender!" cried the sailors.

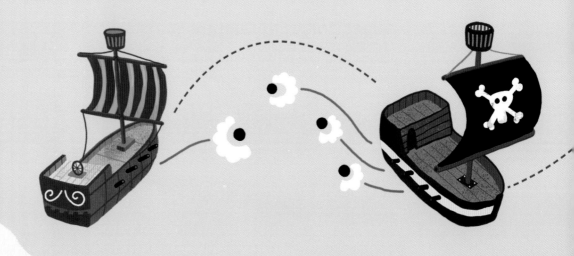

The Pirate King made them all walk the plank and then took their treasure. There were chests filled with diamonds, pearls, rubies, and coins. He stashed it aboard his ship and then set sail for land, to bury his treasure.

At last he spotted an empty beach. It was perfect! The Pirate King got to work. He grabbed his spade and started to dig. Deeper and deeper he went. Then he buried his shining jewels and coins and covered them over with sand.

"Now no other pirates can find my treasure," he said. "Time for me to find a new crew."

The Pirate King set off in his ship. He'd only been sailing for a couple of hours, when he spotted a man in ragged clothes clinging to a broken piece of wood in the water.

"What happened to you?" asked the Pirate King.

"My ship sank," said the man. "Please help me!"

"Would you like to be the first mate on board a pirate ship, under the command of a reckless and daring pirate king?" asked the Pirate King.

The man nodded happily and clambered aboard the ship.

The Pirate King and his first mate sailed on, and they quickly filled the ship with pirates. But meanwhile, rumors of the Pirate King's treasure had spread to a town on the other side of the forest behind the empty beach. People started to search for the jewels and coins.

"Pirates love to bury their treasure," one man said to himself. "If I dig a hole deep enough, I'm sure to find it!"

So, he got a spade, put on his hard hat, and started to dig. He dug a hole so deep and long that it went under the town, under the forest, and toward the beach. He dug and dug, and at last he broke through the golden sand of the beach. But when he climbed out of his hole, he got a big surprise. The Pirate King was standing there glaring at him!

The beach was filled with pirates, and their cutlasses glittered in the sunshine. They roared when they saw the man.

"Look out, me hearties! Thief! Make him walk the plank!" shouted the Pirate King.

The man was terrified. Before the pirates could grab him, he jumped back into the hole, and ran back home, along the tunnel he had made under the forest and the town.

"I'll never mess with pirates again!" he cried.

The Pirate King dug up his treasure, and then he and all his pirates climbed aboard the ship.

"Pull up the anchor!" shouted the Pirate King. "Now I have my crew and my treasure, I can rule the ocean waves again!"

Winnie's Big Egg

It was springtime, and the sun shone brightly over River Farm. Winnie the duck sat on the riverbank and quacked impatiently. She had been sitting on her nest for weeks, but not one of her six eggs had hatched. Winnie shifted around and ruffled her feathers. She turned over her eggs and polished each one. She adored her eggs, but she was beginning to wonder if they would ever hatch. Then, suddenly, there was a CRACK!

Out popped a tiny, fluffy duckling. Winnie was delighted.

Soon the other eggs began to crack, and Winnie was surrounded by five fluffy ducklings. Only the biggest egg remained.

Winnie rolled the big egg beneath her plump chest and warmed it with her soft feathers. She waited and waited, but the egg didn't hatch.

"Why don't you leave it?" suggested the cow. "You have five fine little ducklings. That one is obviously no good."

"No," quacked Winnie, wrapping her wings around the egg.

"I don't think that egg even belongs to you," clucked the wise old chicken, who knew a thing or two about eggs. "It's much too big to be a duck egg."

"Yes," neighed the horse. "I've heard about birds leaving their eggs in other birds' nests. It's a terrible thing."

But Winnie just sat on the last egg and waited.

Then, one sunny afternoon, there was a loud CRACK! Winnie quacked with excitement. All the farm animals gathered around to see the new arrival.

"I bet it's a baby goose," whispered the chicken.

"I think it will be a baby swan," neighed the horse.

Everyone held their breath as out popped ... two tiny ducklings. It was twins! Winnie quacked with pride. She had always known the big egg was special. Now she had seven perfect little ducklings.

"Come on, boys and girls," she called as she proudly led her babies down to the river.

The Duck with the Golden Eggs

A long time ago, a poor old man and woman lived in a little hut with their son. One evening, when they were down to their last crust of bread, they wondered how they were going to survive. Suddenly, an elf appeared on the table.

"Go to the village pond and catch the duck there," said the elf. "Bring her home then wait for her to lay an egg."

The next day, the old man did as he was told. He took the duck back to the hut, then he, his wife, and their son waited eagerly for an egg to appear.

Suddenly, with a soft quack, the duck laid a golden egg.

The poor family couldn't believe their eyes.

"I will sell the egg to buy some food," cried the old man.

Day after day, the duck laid more golden eggs, and soon the old man and his family had lots of money and grew very rich.

The story of the golden eggs spread far and wide. One day, a neighbor, who was jealous of their wealth, came to the house to try and trick the old woman into giving him the duck.

When he picked it up, he saw some words written in gold beneath the duck's wing. It said: "Whoever eats this duck will become king!"

"Dear lady," said the sly neighbor, "I'm so hungry. Could you spare me some food? Perhaps we might share this duck?"

The old woman said she couldn't possibly cook the duck as it had brought them such good fortune. But eventually, she felt sorry for the man and gave in.

"Let's go find some vegetables while it's cooking," said the man. "Then we can have a feast."

The old woman and the man left the house. While they were out, the son returned home from work. The delicious aroma of roast duck filled the house. The son was hungry, so he took the duck out of the oven, and ate the whole bird.

When the old man came home and discovered what had happened, he threw his son out of the house in anger.

The son wandered for many days, until he came to a city, where the king had just died. The king had no children, and so the people had declared that the next person to walk through the city gates would rule their land.

As the son walked into the city, the crowd cheered in delight.

The son was a kind and wise ruler and, as he had a forgiving nature, he asked his parents, who were poor once again, to come and live in the palace with him. There, they all lived happily until the end of their days.

Clever Jackal Gets Away

One day Jackal was trotting through a narrow, rocky pass, looking for something to eat, when he saw Lion coming toward him.

Jackal was filled with fear. He had played so many tricks on Lion in the past, he was sure that Lion wouldn't miss this opportunity to take his revenge. In a flash, Jackal thought of a cunning plan.

"Oh, great Lion—help!" he cried, looking up at the rocks above his head. "See that huge rock above us? It's about to fall and we shall both be crushed. Please save us!"

Lion looked up, in alarm. Before he had time to think, Lion was using his great strength to hold up the overhanging rock.

"Oh, thank you, great King!" yelped Jackal. "I will fetch that log over there to hold up the rock!"

And with that, he ran away, leaving Lion holding the rock that wasn't going to fall at all!

Thunder and Lightning

A long time ago, Thunder and Lightning lived on Earth among the people.

Thunder was an old mother sheep, and Lightning was her only son, a ram. Whenever the ram got angry he would go on a rampage, knocking down trees and causing trouble. When he did these terrible things, his mother would shout at him to stop in a very loud, rumbling voice. But Lightning didn't listen. He still caused damage whenever he was in a bad mood.

At last the people of the land couldn't stand it any more, and they complained to their king.

The king banished both Thunder and Lightning from the Earth and made them live in the sky.

Lightning still gets angry and tries to cause destruction; that's why you can see light flashing across the sky in a storm. And Thunder continues to shout at him, her booming voice following after the flash of light.

The Penguin Who Wanted to Sparkle

One moonlit night, Mommy Penguin's egg went CRACK! A tiny beak appeared, a head, then two wings and two orange feet. A fluffy little penguin chick called Pip hopped out.

"Pretty sparkles!" she squeaked, as she gazed up at the sparkly stars in the sky. Then Pip saw a funny fish leap out of the ocean waves—SPLASH! It was all shiny and sparkly. "I want to sparkle, too," she squeaked.

Soon it began to snow. Pip watched the sparkling snowflakes floating down. "If I catch some, I can sprinkle them on my feathers," she thought. "Then I will sparkle, too."

Pip ran around, trying to catch the snowflakes, but they just melted on her wings. Then she found a bank of powdery white snow, twinkling in the moonlight. "Now I will sparkle!" she cried, rolling over in the snowy drift.

But the moon disappeared behind a cloud, and Pip's feathers didn't sparkle one tiny bit.

"Maybe I can catch a sparkly star," thought Pip, jumping up and down. But she couldn't reach one, no matter how hard she tried.

"What are you doing, Pip?" asked the other penguins.

"I'm trying to catch some sparkles," Pip explained.

Just then a friendly whale swam by. "All that jumping and rolling around looks very tiring!" he laughed. "Why don't you come and slide on my back instead?"

Everyone agreed that this was a wonderful idea—even Pip. One by one, the penguins whooshed down the whale's back and landed in the glittering sea. SPLASH! Pip hopped out and shook her wet feathers in the sunshine.

"Look!" cried the other penguins. "You're sparkling all over!"

"So that's how you sparkle," cried Pip, dancing in the snow. "By having fun in the sun. Come on, everyone. Let's do it again!"

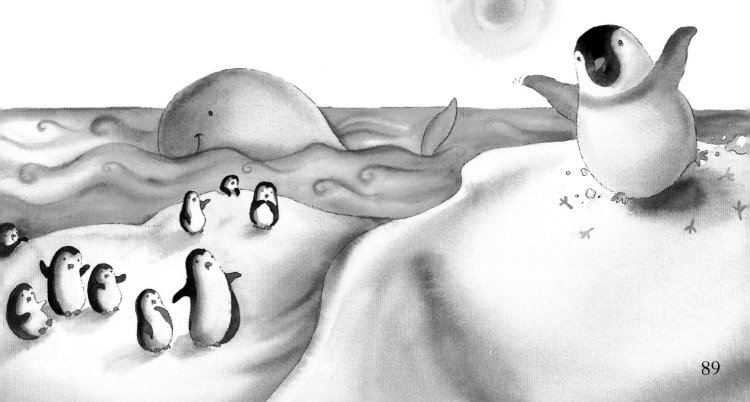

Mars the Pony

Once upon a time there was a pony called Mars. He lived in a riding school with lots of other ponies. Mars was too young to be ridden, so he stayed in the field all day while all the other ponies taught little boys and girls to ride. Mars was very happy. He loved munching on grass. He loved jumping the fences put up for the bigger horses to jump. But best of all he loved being groomed and cuddled by all the boys and girls.

Mars was very happy with his life until, one day, one of the grooms put a bridle on him.

"It's time for your training to begin," she whispered, rubbing him kindly on the nose. "Soon you will be ridden like all the other ponies."

"Oh, goody!" thought Mars. "Being ridden looks easy. I'm sure I'll be really good at it."

But Mars couldn't have been more wrong. Being ridden wasn't at all easy. And he wasn't very good at it. In fact, having a person on your back was rather scary. It made him feel all wobbly and unbalanced. And the world outside his field was full of terrifying things, like noisy tractors, screaming children, and, worst of all, plastic bags that flapped in the wind.

Mars really wished that he didn't have to be ridden. He wished that everyone would just leave him alone in his field. So one night, he came up with a plan. He wouldn't let anyone ride him.

The next morning, when one of the grooms tried to catch him, he put back his ears, kicked up his hooves, and raced away. After that he tried to kick or bite anyone who came near him. Soon no one dared approach him and Mars was left well alone. At first, Mars was very pleased with himself. But soon he began to feel rather lonely. He didn't know what to do. He didn't want to be ridden, but he did miss being groomed and cuddled.

Then one night, as Mars was dozing in his field, something magical happened. A dazzling white horse appeared before him.

"Don't be afraid," whispered the horse. "I am your guardian angel. I have come to help you. Follow me!"

In an instant, the white horse whirled around and soared into the sky. Mars galloped after him. They galloped across the night sky until they came to a field.

"Look down," said the white horse kindly.

Mars looked down and saw a small pony leaping easily over a jump with a little girl on his back. Mars blinked and neighed with amazement. That pony was him. But who was that girl who was riding on his back?

"That's Katy," said the white horse gently, as if reading his thoughts. "See how gentle and kind she is. She would never hurt you."

Mars stared and stared until everything turned into a misty blur before his eyes. Then he suddenly blinked and found himself back in his own field at the riding stables. The white horse had vanished and he was alone once more.

"Oh," sighed Mars sadly. "It must have been a dream."

He couldn't stop thinking about the kind little girl he had seen.

The following morning, Mars was hiding in the corner of his field when a little girl came to the gate.

"Hello Mars," she called, waving a carrot in his direction. Mars crept out from his hiding place and stared. It was the girl from the dream. It was Katy!

Katy climbed the gate and walked slowly toward Mars, taking care not to frighten him.

"Come on, boy," she whispered softly. "I won't hurt you." Then she stood still and waited.

At first, Mars refused to budge. Then his curiosity got the better of him and he crept slowly toward her. Still she didn't move. Suddenly, Mars felt quite brave. He walked slowly up to Katy's shoulder and lowered his head. Katy put out her hand and stroked his head. Then she gave him the carrot. As Mars crunched the carrot, Katy gently put a head collar over his head.

"There you go, boy," she said softly.

After that, Mars always allowed Katy to catch him. And soon he even let her sit on his back. By the end of the summer he and Katy were the very best of friends and sailed over jumps together. And when the stables held their summer show, guess who won the jumping competition? Mars, of course.

Thanks to the mysterious white horse, Mars had allowed himself to trust again.

Super Max!

Max was a very small boy with a very BIG secret. Whenever he ate ice cream, something amazing happened. A red cape appeared, his shoes turned into blue boots and a yellow mask covered his eyes. "I'm not Max any more!" he shouted. "I'm SUPER MAX!"

Super Max could fly to the moon and back in three minutes. He could lift skyscrapers with one finger and he had X-ray vision. Each night, he turned back into Max, until the next time he ate ice cream.

One day after a bowl of strawberry swirl, Super Max was playing on the moon. Suddenly a spaceship WHOOSHED past, out of control! The astronauts were worried. But Super Max didn't panic. He zoomed after the spaceship and guided it safely back to Earth.

"Our hero!" cheered the astronauts. "How can we thank you, Super Max?"

"That's easy," said Super Max with a grin. "Just buy me an ice cream!"

Super Shoes

Luke's dad invented all sorts of peculiar things, but his latest invention was the strangest yet.

"Special shoes!" he said, as Luke put them on. "I want you to try them out for a day and tell me what you think."

"What do they do?" asked Luke.

"You'll see," said his dad.

At first, Luke's friends laughed.

"You look silly!" they said. "Those shoes aren't cool!"

But they soon changed their minds when they saw what the shoes could do. In gym class, the springs in the heels made Luke leap the highest. In the playground, roller-skate wheels popped out of the soles. Later on, a shower of candy burst from the toes! By the end of the school day, all Luke's friends wanted a pair.

"Sorry Luke," his dad chuckled. "My inventions are only for you. I have just invented a jacket with wings. Will you wear it to school tomorrow?"

"Definitely!" said Luke.

Prince Kindhearted

Once upon a time, there lived a very clever and kind prince. Throughout the kingdom, he was known as Prince Kindhearted.

Prince Kindhearted wanted to travel so that he could learn more about the world and become a wiser and better man. The king gave the prince his finest horse and his best servant, and they set off with the prince.

As they traveled across the fields, the prince saw a huge eagle chasing a beautiful swan through the sky. He took out his bow and aimed it at the eagle.

"Oh, thank you, kind prince," cried the swan happily. "I'm the enchanted daughter of the Knight Invisible. You have just saved me from the terrible sorcerer King Koshchey. If you're ever in need, just call out "Knight Invisible" three times, and my father will come to your aid." And with that the swan disappeared.

The prince and the servant continued on their journey. They traveled across mountains and rivers, and through many kingdoms, until they came to a large desert.

"Look! There's a well," said Prince Kindhearted to the servant. "I'll lower you down on a rope so you can get us some water to drink."

"I'm far too heavy," replied the servant. "Let me lower you down instead."

So the prince went into the well. When he had scooped up some water, he called out for his servant to pull him up again.

"No, I won't!" shouted the servant. "You've always lived a life of luxury, while I've always done what other people told me to do. I will only get you out if you agree to swap places with me. I shall be the prince and you shall be my servant."

The prince didn't want to die in the well, so he agreed. He swapped his horse and clothes with the servant, and the pair continued on their journey.

Several days later they came to a palace. The pretend prince went up to the king and asked to marry his daughter.

"You may marry the princess," replied the king, "if you can defeat my enemies. They are sending in their army tomorrow."

The pretend prince agreed. He took Prince Kindhearted to one side and said, "Go out tomorrow and defeat the army. If you succeed, I will release you from your duties and you can return to your father's kingdom."

So, the next morning, Prince Kindhearted left the palace. In a quiet voice, he called out "Knight Invisible" three times. Suddenly, a magnificent knight appeared before him.

"I will help you defeat the army," said the Knight Invisible.

The knight raced off toward the enemy army.

In no time at all, the knight and Prince Kindhearted won the battle, and Prince Kindhearted returned to the palace.

However, the princess had overheard the pretend prince talking with Prince Kindhearted and had seen the real prince ride out to battle. When the pretend prince tried to claim her hand in marriage, she cried out, "Father, he is not a real prince. This man here fought the battle and he is the true prince. I will marry only him!"

The king was very angry. "You shall be punished for this," he shouted to the servant.

But Prince Kindhearted, being the kind man he was, asked the king to forgive the servant. The servant left the palace to seek his fortune elsewhere, and Prince Kindhearted and the princess were married and lived happily ever after.

Little Dragon

Little Dragon was reading a book all about a nasty man in a tin suit who fought little dragons with his sword. Little Dragon felt all worried and wobbly. Just then, he heard voices.

"Oh, no!" thought Little Dragon. "Dragon fighters!" And he hid under his blanket.

Outside, Princess Pippa, Prince Pip, and Little Baron Boris were walking up the hill. Boris was making a lot of noise and waving a toy sword.

"Let's go on a dragon hunt," said Boris. "Are you coming?"

"No, thank you," said Pippa and Pip.

"Scaredy cats, scaredy cats!" sang Boris.

"We are not scaredy cats!" said Pip angrily.

"Look!" cried Boris. "Dragon footprints!"

They followed the footprints right up to Little Dragon's door.

"Er … you two go first," said Boris. "I'll stand outside and guard the door in case the dragon tries to escape."

Pip and Pippa pushed the door open. It was very dark and spooky inside the cave. They saw a light, and a big shadow that looked like … a dragon! They were very frightened!

"Who's there?" asked Pip bravely.

"It's me!" said Little Dragon.

"Are you a dragon?" asked Pippa.

"Yes," said Little Dragon.

"You're very small," said Pippa.

"I'm big on the inside," said Little Dragon, standing on tippy toes. Then he started to cry.

"Are you going to fight me now, like in my book?" he sniffed.

"Of course not," said Pippa, and she gave him a big hug.

"Let's just be friends," said Prince Pip. So that was settled.

"Would you like a snack?" asked Little Dragon.

"Oh, yes, please!" said Pippa and Pip. Little Dragon fetched a plate of cakes.

"Does your noisy friend with the pointy stick want one?" asked Little Dragon.

"Oh, you mean Boris," said Pippa. "I'm sure he'd like one. He's always hungry!"

"Would you like a cake, Boris?" asked Little Dragon.

"It's a dragon!" cried Little Baron Boris, running away.

"Now who's a scaredy cat?" laughed Pip.

Soon it was time for Pip and Pippa to go.

"Can we be friends tomorrow?" asked Little Dragon.

"We'll be friends forever," said Pip and Pippa.

The Musicians of Bremen

Once upon a time, a farmer had a donkey. The animal had worked hard for him for many long years, but now he was old and unfit.

"You work too slowly," said the farmer. "I don't want you any more." And he sent the donkey away.

Although the donkey felt sad, he decided to make the most of his freedom. He had always wanted to be a musician, so he set off for the town of Bremen to start his new career.

He hadn't walked far when he found a dog lying on the road, panting hard.

"What's wrong, my friend?" asked the donkey.

"My master sent me away because I am old and weak and can no longer hunt," puffed the dog. "But how can an old mutt like me earn a living?"

"Why don't you join me," said the donkey. "I'm going to Bremen to become a musician."

The dog agreed to go with the donkey and they set off to town together.

After they had walked a short distance, they saw a cat. She was meowing sorrowfully.

"What's wrong?" asked the donkey. "You sound so sad."

"My mistress has sent me away because I'm too old to catch mice any more."

"Come with us to Bremen," said the donkey. "You sing beautifully and will make a fine musician."

The cat thought it sounded like a splendid idea and decided to join them.

It was getting dark when they met a rooster, crowing mournfully with all his might.

"What's wrong?" asked the donkey.

"My master wanted to give me to the butcher," cried the rooster. "So I ran away."

"Come with us. We're off to town to become musicians. You can sing with us," said the donkey.

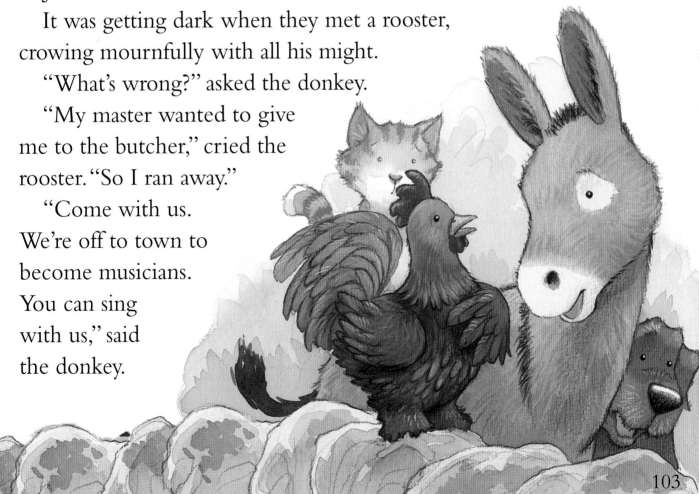

The four friends carried on down the road. It was late at night when they came to a little cottage at the edge of the forest. They were tired and hungry, so they decided to see if they could shelter there for the night.

They went to the window and peered in. Sitting around a table laden with food and money was a gang of thieves.

The friends knew they would never share their food or shelter, so they thought up a clever plan for getting rid of the thieves.

The donkey put his front hooves on the window ledge. The dog jumped on his back. The cat climbed on the dog's back. And, last of all, the rooster perched upon the cat's head. Then, in their loudest voices, they began to sing, before bursting through the window. The thieves, who thought that some terrible monster had come for them, ran away into the forest as fast as they could.

Laughing, the four friends sat down at the table and ate all the delicious food. Then, after such a long and exciting day, since they were all very tired, they turned out the lights and searched for a bed.

The donkey lay down on some straw in the yard.

The dog lay on the mat beside the door.

The cat curled up in front of the fire.

And the rooster perched on top of the chimney.

The four friends were very happy to have found a new home, so they decided to stay in the cottage.

I expect that they are still there now, and if you stand outside their windows, you'll probably hear them practicing their singing!

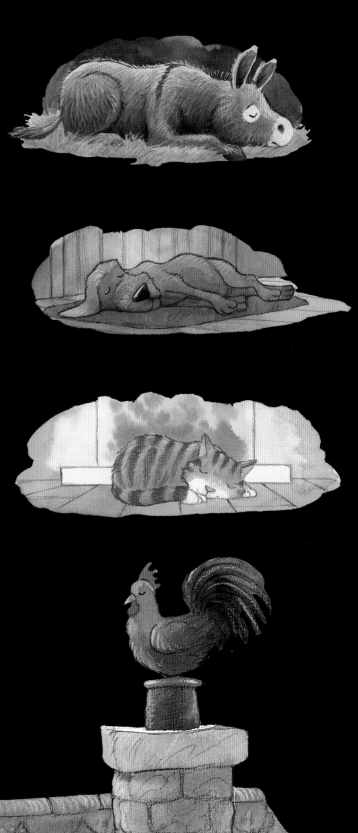

Flamingo's Dance Class

Flamingo was a very elegant bird. She never tripped over or bumped into things. But the other animals in the jungle weren't always so graceful.

"Look out!" Flamingo exclaimed as Elephant barged into a tree.

"Be careful!" she cried when Hippo wiped mud on her feathers.

"Watch your step!" she squeaked as Crocodile trampled over her toes. "You're all so clumsy!"

Elephant, Hippo, and Crocodile felt embarrassed. They didn't want the other animals to think they were clumsy.

"A ballet lesson will help," said Flamingo.

First, she showed her class how to do a pirouette.

"Now it's your turn," she said.

Elephant did her best, but she was so heavy that she just drilled a hole deep into the ground and got her leg stuck.

"Perhaps a pirouette is too hard," said Flamingo. "Try this instead."

She stood on one leg in a beautiful pose, and tucked the other leg under her body. Hippo tried to copy her, but he accidentally kicked a tree and knocked it down. Flamingo groaned.

"Perhaps you would be more graceful if you looked daintier," she said, handing them some tutus. "Try these on."

But poor Crocodile's belly was so low to the ground that his tutu dragged in the mud.

"I don't think we'll ever be as elegant as you, Flamingo," said Elephant sadly.

Flamingo sighed and looked at her friends. Elephant could use her trunk to pick leaves and berries gently. Hippo dived underwater without bumping into anything, and when Crocodile glided into the swamp he didn't make a single ripple.

Suddenly, Flamingo felt very silly. Why was she trying to change her friends? When they acted naturally, they all looked graceful.

"I'm sorry I called you clumsy," she said. "You're perfect just the way you are!"

The Three Feathers

Once upon a time, there was an old king who had three sons. The two older boys were confident and loved to boast, while the youngest son was quiet and shy.

The king loved all his sons equally, and he didn't know which one to leave his kingdom to when he was gone. So he decided to set them a challenge.

"Whoever brings me the finest carpet shall be king after my death," he said. Then he threw three feathers into the air. "Wherever they fly, so each way one of you will go."

One feather went east, one went west, and the last one flew straight ahead, landing on the ground near the castle.

"We'll go east and west," laughed the older sons, thinking that their brother wouldn't find a carpet by the castle.

The youngest son sat down and wondered what to do. Suddenly, he noticed a trap door in the ground. He opened it and climbed down some steps into a dark hole.

Sitting by a large chest was a big toad.

The young boy plucked up his courage and said, "Please, Mr. Toad, can you help me find the finest carpet in the kingdom?"

The toad opened the chest and gave the boy the finest carpet he had ever seen.

When the king saw the beautiful carpet, he was amazed. "The kingdom shall go to you, my youngest son," he declared.

The two older brothers were angry and jealous. They begged their father to set another challenge.

The old king gave in and said, "Whoever brings me the most beautiful ring shall rule my kingdom."

Once again, the king threw three feathers into the air. The same thing happened, and the two older boys went east and west, while the youngest son stood in front of the castle.

When his brothers had gone, he went through the trap door.

"Please, Mr. Toad, I need to find the most beautiful ring."

The toad grinned at the young boy. He opened the chest and pulled out a sparkling ring, covered in precious jewels.

When the king saw the ring, he couldn't believe his eyes. "You, my youngest son, shall rule my kingdom."

The two older sons were even more annoyed and asked their father to set another task, but this time he didn't give in.

When the king died, the youngest son took his place. He was a brave ruler, full of kindness (especially toward toads).

The Ant and the Grasshopper

One sunny day, a grasshopper was hopping and chirping happily in a field. An ant passed by, carrying food to his nest.

"Come and play with me," cried the grasshopper. "It's too hot to work. You can gather food some other day."

"I'm gathering food now for the winter," replied the ant. "There will be no food then. You should do the same."

"Don't be silly!" laughed the grasshopper. "There'll be plenty!"

The seasons changed. It grew cold and started to rain. The grasshopper was hungry. Shivering and wet, he hopped from place to place looking for something to eat.

Then he met the ant again. The ant was having his dinner.

"Where did you get that food?" cried the grasshopper.

"I gathered it when the sun was shining," replied the ant.

The grasshopper felt sad. "You were right," he sighed. "I should have gathered some food when I had the chance."

And the moral of the story is: it's best to be prepared for hard days ahead.

Two Men and the Bear

One day two men were walking through the forest when they came across a bear. Both men were scared. One man scampered up a nearby tree to hide. The other man wasn't quick enough. He knew there was nothing he could do to escape, so he dropped to the ground and played dead.

The bear came over to the man on the ground and sniffed him around his ears. The man was terrified, but the bear walked away.

As soon as the bear had gone, the other man jumped down from his hiding place.

"What did the bear say to you?" he asked.

"It said I should think about whether you're really a friend," the man answered. "You only cared about yourself and jumped in the tree without a thought for me!"

And the moral of the story is: friendship is tested in times of trouble.

Doctor Finley Pig

Finley was a very happy pig. He spent his days sunbathing in the mud. Life just couldn't be better.

"It's all right for you!" said Agatha Chicken, who was always sticking her beak in other people's business. "This is a busy farm, lazybones," she clucked.

"I'm not a lazybones," replied the happy little pig. "I'm Finley."

"Don't talk back!" Agatha flapped her wings and squawked until Finley ran away.

Finley sat under a tree to think. Taking mud baths was a lovely way to spend your time, but he did want to be a big help on the busy farm too. What would he be good at?

Mommy Pig was puzzled. "Where are you going with all those things, Finley?" she asked.

"I'm not Finley, I'm Doctor Pig!" replied Finley. "And I'm late for my first patient. What seems to be the trouble, Mrs. Moo?"

Mrs. Moo mooed. "Don't say moo, say ahhh!" said Finley.

"Finley, there's nothing wrong with my leg," said Mrs. Moo, as Finley tried to tie a bandage around it.

"Hold still for Doctor Pig, please!" said Finley.

Chester Sheep was not good at having his heart listened to. He wouldn't stop munching.

The geese, Heidi and Dora, refused their medicine.

And Tilly the sheepdog? Well, she just ran away ...

Being a doctor was really hard work, but the most difficult patients of all were the chickens. There were just so many of them, and they all wanted to be first in line.

At the end of a long day, Mommy Pig was pleased to see Finley.

"I'm very good at being a doctor," said Finley. "But I'm even better at being me."

Life just couldn't be better!

The Emperor's New Clothes

Many years ago there was a wealthy and proud emperor who only cared about fashion. Instead of spending time attending to his royal duties, he wasted hours in his private chambers, parading up and down in fancy outfits, admiring himself from every angle in all the mirrors that lined the walls.

The emperor's extravagant tastes soon became famous far and wide. Merchants came to the city, hoping to sell him clothes. But even their finest wares didn't satisfy the emperor for long.

One morning, when the emperor was in a meeting with the prime minister, two strangers called at the palace.

"Your Majesty, we are master weavers," declared the taller of the two men. "Our clothes are created from the rarest fabric."

"But only the lucky few will be able to enjoy the true marvel of our creation," said the other man.

"Only the lucky few?" asked the emperor.

The two men looked at each other. "Our fabrics are so special, only the cleverest people can even see them. To anyone else, they're simply invisible. It's like there's nothing there at all!"

The prime minister started to protest at the idea, but the emperor silenced him with a wave of his hand.

"Give these fine gentlemen everything they need," said the emperor. "I want them to make me a splendid new outfit for my royal procession next week."

As the prime minister handed the two weavers twelve bags of gold, he thought that he saw them wink at each other.

A few days later, the emperor called for the prime minister.

"Go and find out how the weavers are getting on with my new suit," he cried impatiently.

The prime minister went off to see the weavers. When he entered their workshop, all he could see was an empty loom.

"What do you think?" asked the small weaver. "Look at the fabric—isn't it divine?"

The prime minister's heart sank. He couldn't see anything, but he didn't want to appear foolish.

"It's a triumph," he lied. "I shall be sure to tell the emperor what I've seen."

The day of the royal procession finally arrived. The weavers came to the emperor's chamber.

"Your Majesty," said the tall weaver, bowing. "We present your new clothes!"

The emperor made a startled squeal. He couldn't see anything. He looked at the prime minister to see what he thought. He seemed to be gazing in admiration at the new outfit.

"Thank you!" he said, too proud to admit he couldn't see anything. "It's perfect!"

People had gathered in the streets to catch a glimpse of the emperor in his new suit. For just one second the crowd went silent. Then, since no one wanted to look foolish, they cheered.

Just then, a small boy pushed to the front of the crowd.

"The emperor doesn't have any clothes on!" he called out, and the crowd erupted with laughter.

The emperor gulped. The weavers, who were right now sneaking off with his gold, had made him look like a fool.

Filled with shame, the emperor vowed that he would never again be so vain about his clothes!

I'll Have to Think Again

Frog was sitting on a lily pad, reading a cookbook. It was his birthday and he wanted to make a birthday cake to surprise his friends. He wrote a list of the ingredients, and set out to get them.

First Frog went to his friend, the miller, to get a bag of flour.

"How will you get the flour home?" asked the miller.

"I'll swim up the river with it," replied Frog.

"But the flour will get wet," warned the miller, "and it will be no use to you at all."

"Oh," said Frog. "I'll have to think again."

Next, Frog went to see his friend, Brown Cow, for a bucket of her milk.

"How will you get the milk home without spilling it into the river?" asked Brown Cow.

"Oh, I don't really know," mumbled Frog. "I'll have to think again."

Frog decided to visit Speckled Hen for some eggs.

"Take as many as you need," she told Frog, "but how will you get them home?"

"I'll tuck the eggs under my chin," said Frog, happily.

"But you might drop them and then they'll break," replied Speckled Hen.

"Oh," croaked Frog, and a tear fell from the corner of his eye. "I'll just have to think again."

Frog returned to his lily pad, empty-handed and miserable. The sun was warm and he was tired, so he drifted off to sleep.

"Happy birthday to you …"

Suddenly, Frog woke up. On the bank of the pond stood all his friends, singing. The miller was holding a birthday cake.

"But … how?" gasped Frog.

"We wanted to surprise you," said the miller. "Brown Cow provided the milk, Speckled Hen laid some eggs, and I mixed the ingredients with my flour and baked you a cake."

"Thank you!" grinned Frog. "But I was going to make a cake to surprise you."

"Well," his friends laughed, "you'll have to think again!"

Fire Flyer

Ben was the oldest engine in the fire station. He should have been happy, because he loved his job. But lately, all the newer engines had been getting to the fires first.

"I haven't put out a fire for ages," Ben told his friend Harry Helicopter. "The town is always full of cars, and the newer engines zip through the traffic much quicker than I can."

Harry thought hard. Then he flashed his lights. "I have an idea," he exclaimed. "Flying is much quicker than driving. If you could fly to the fires, you'd always get there first."

"But how can a fire engine fly?" Ben asked. "It's impossible. Engines don't have wings."

"I'll carry you," said Harry. "I'm strong, and I'll get you to the fire quickly."

Suddenly, the fire alarm started to ring. Ben felt worried. He had never flown before, but he really wanted to put out the fire, so he let Harry lift him up. Soon they were whizzing across town, high above the narrow streets and traffic jams.

"There's the fire!" Ben cried.

A huge factory was engulfed in flames. SPLOOSH! SQUIRT! Ben used his hose to put out the fire, and then Harry lowered him to the ground.

The newer fire engines raced up to the factory. "Thank goodness you got here so fast!" they gasped. "That fire was spreading quickly."

The fire officers gave Ben and Harry three cheers. "From now on, we'll always keep Harry nearby to make sure that Ben can reach the fires," they said. "Three cheers for brave Ben and Harry!"

The Cursed Princess

There was once a young man, named Thomas, who was given a special horn from his dying father.

"Son, I shall not be here for much longer," sighed the old man. "I want you to have this horn. If you place it to your ear, you will be able to hear other people's thoughts."

A few days later, the old man died. Thomas was very sad.

"There is nothing left for me here," he sighed. "I will travel for a while and look for some work."

He took the horn and packed the rest of his belongings, then set off on his journey. After traveling for many days, Thomas arrived at a huge castle. The owner of the castle was a giant with long golden hair. Although Thomas felt afraid of the giant, he asked if he could give him any work.

"You can stay and make my meals," roared the giant.

So Thomas unpacked his things and prepared some supper.

One day, when he went down into the cellar to get some flour to make bread, he heard someone crying. In a dark corner, he found a young girl.

"Who are you?" asked Thomas. "Why are you down here?"

The girl replied, "I'm a princess. The giant killed my father, locked me up, and cursed our castle. Please help."

Thomas felt very sorry for the girl, but he didn't see how he could overpower the huge giant. Suddenly he had an idea.

"Don't worry," he told the weeping girl. "I will help."

Thomas went back up to the kitchen. That evening, when he took the giant his supper, Thomas took out his horn. As soon as the giant was busy eating his food, Thomas put the horn to his ear and listened to the giant's thoughts.

"I think my cook knows about the princess," thought the giant. "Tomorrow, I will eat him for breakfast. He must never find out that the secret to my strength is my long golden hair."

Thomas did not want to be the giant's breakfast! So, later that night, he crept into the giant's bedroom and cut off his long golden hair.

When the giant woke the next morning, he felt very weak. He saw all his golden hair lying by his bed and knew that he wouldn't have the strength to eat Thomas. Quickly, he grabbed his belongings and fled from the castle.

As soon as Thomas saw the giant running away, he climbed down to the cellar and released the princess. The giant's curse was lifted and the castle went back to its magnificent self. Thomas and the princess fell in love and were soon married.

The Fox and the Goat

One hot day, a thirsty fox was searching for something to drink. At last he found a well in a farmyard. He stuck his nose over the edge, but the water was too far down. Very carefully, he balanced on the side, trying to reach the cool, clear water. But though his nose was so close that he could smell it, he still couldn't quite reach the water.

The fox made one last try, stretching out his tongue with all his might. SPLASH! he toppled right in.

The sides of the well were so slippery that when the fox tried to climb out, he just kept sliding back down. He was stuck!

After a while, a goat came by looking for a drink. He was surprised to see the fox in the water.

"What on earth are you doing down there?" he asked.

"Just cooling down," replied the fox. "The water in this well is the best for miles around. Why don't you jump in and try it?"

The goat was very hot and thirsty, and the water did look very refreshing, so he jumped in to join the fox.

"You're right!" said the goat, taking a long drink and relaxing in the water. "It's lovely and cool down here."

Soon the goat decided that it was time to go on his way.

"How do we get out?" he asked.

"That is a bit of a problem," the fox admitted.

"But I have an idea. If you stick your legs out, you can wedge yourself in the well. Then I can climb on your back and jump out."

"That's all very well, but what about me?" the goat bleated.

"Once I've climbed out, I can help you," the fox explained.

So the goat wedged himself against the walls of the well and the fox clambered on to his back and leaped out.

"Thank you," laughed the fox, as he turned to leave.

"Hold on! What about me? How am I going to get out?" cried the goat.

"You should have thought about that before you jumped in," replied the sly fox, and off he ran.

And the moral of the story is: always look before you leap.

In My Airplane

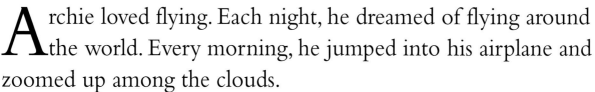

Archie loved flying. Each night, he dreamed of flying around the world. Every morning, he jumped into his airplane and zoomed up among the clouds.

"Wheee!" he shouted, looping the loop. "This is the best feeling in the world!" There was only one problem. His flying adventures never lasted long enough! School and homework always got in the way. So one weekend, Archie decided to make his dreams come true.

"I'm going on an adventure," he said. "This weekend, I'm going to fly farther than I've ever flown before."

At midnight, Archie packed some food and a change of clothes, and climbed into his airplane. His mom and dad were asleep, but his sister waved to him from her bedroom window.

Whoosh! Archie's airplane shot up into the sky.

"Look out, world," he shouted. "Here we come!"

In the distance, Archie could see the ocean sparkling in the moonlight. "I wonder if there are any pirates at sea," he said. The airplane flew out over the foamy waves. Soon he spotted a ship cutting through the water. A Jolly Roger flag fluttered from the highest mast and a pirate sat in the lookout. Archie waved from his airplane.

"Avast, me hearties!" the pirate roared. "A pirate in the sky!"

The pirates aimed their cannons at the airplane, but Archie was miles away before they could fire!

Archie zoomed over playful dolphins, leaping fish, and giant octopuses. He saw desert islands with palm trees waving in the breeze. Then he reached land again, and zoomed over cities, towns, and fields, until he saw a fairground.

"Awesome!" Archie cried. He landed his airplane and ran off to explore. There were lots of rides, but something was missing.

"There's no Ferris wheel!" said a little girl sadly. "I want to go up high."

Archie smiled. "I've got an idea," he said.

He went back to his airplane.

"Step right up!" he shouted in his loudest voice. "Free rides on the best little airplane in the world!"

Soon there was a line
of people stretching all around
the fairground, waiting for a ride on
the little airplane. Archie gave everyone a ride, and
when the fairground closed, he flew on until he
came to the highest mountains he had ever seen.
They were topped with snow, and the sun was
dazzling. Archie spiraled around the mountaintops.

"They look like ice cream," he said. "This is
making me hungry!"

Just then, Archie spotted a little café at the very top
of the highest mountain. He landed his airplane and
ordered a hot chocolate with marshmallows and golden
sprinkles. The sun was setting and the stars were starting to
twinkle. Archie yawned.

"Maybe it's time to go home," he said. But he had been
flying for so long that he couldn't remember the way. "I wish I'd
brought a map. Come on, little airplane. Let's just keep flying
and see what we find."

In his little airplane, Archie zoomed over a busy city.
"I recognize these streets," he said. Then he saw someone
waving at him. It was his mom, dad, and sister. Archie had flown
all the way around the world until he arrived back home!

You're Too Little!

Bobby loved being the baby of the family. It was fun to play with his big brothers. The only thing that he didn't like was being left behind when his brothers went exploring.

"You're too little to come," they said each time. "Wait till you're bigger." So while they were gone, Bobby thought of jokes to cheer himself up.

One day, when his brothers were out exploring, Bobby's tummy started to rumble.

"I'm hungry," he said, looking around.

There were lots of leaves on the trees, but the branches were all too high. Little Bobby stretched his trunk as far as he could, but he couldn't even touch the lowest leaf. A tear rolled down Bobby's cheek.

Then a cheerful voice said, "Don't cry, Bobby!"

He turned around and saw his brothers stomping toward him.

"Just hold on to my tail," said one of them. "We'll take you to the tastiest food in the jungle."

Bobby stomped into the jungle with his brothers. They led him through prickly undergrowth and past sparkling watering holes. Bobby started singing, and his brothers joined in.

At last they reached a low tree, with bright-green leaves at just the right height for a little elephant. Bobby used his trunk to pick a bunch of them, and pushed them into his mouth. Yum, yum! When he was full, he told his brothers all his best jokes, and they laughed until they cried.

"Can I always come with you on your adventures?" Bobby asked.

His brothers wrapped their trunks around him and laughed. "Of course you can," they said. "It's much more fun with you here!"

Rabbit's New Friend

Edward the rabbit loved nighttime. He lived on a grassy hill next to a little forest. When the moon rose, he snuggled into his cozy tree-trunk den, opened his favorite book, and read by the light of the stars. He loved listening to the owls hooting and the chirps of the grasshoppers.

The stories in his book were all about friends having adventures, and sometimes he wondered what that would be like.

"It might be fun to have a friend," he thought. But he never saw any other rabbits on the hill. So he just read his book and dreamed of playing games.

One night, Edward was reading his book as usual when something bright and sparkling landed next to him with a fizzing noise. It was followed by another … and another!

"What is it?" Edward cried. He looked up, and saw that some of the brightest stars were falling out of the sky. As he watched, the falling stars clustered together into the shape of a rabbit.

"Hello," said the star rabbit. "Want to play?"

Edward hopped out of his den. "Yes please!" he exclaimed.

The two rabbits played every game they could think of. They ran and chased and dug. They bounced and hopped and giggled. They ate all the carrots that Edward had in his den.

"I never knew it could be so much fun to have a friend," said Edward. "What shall we play next?"

"Hide and seek," said the star rabbit, and his eyes sparkled with mischief. "I'll hide."

Edward covered his eyes and counted to ten. When he looked, the star rabbit was nowhere to be seen. "Ready or not, here I come!" Edward called. He searched through the long grass, behind tree trunks and inside fallen logs, but there was no star rabbit.

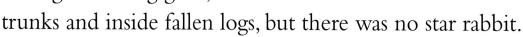

Then he remembered his little den. He peered inside and saw a white, tufty tail.

"Found you!" he cried in delight.

The rabbit quickly hopped out of the den, but it wasn't the star rabbit. It was a white rabbit, and she was shivering.

"I got lost and I needed somewhere to rest," said the white rabbit. "My name is Sylvie."

"Would you like to play hide and seek, and meet my friend the star rabbit?" said Edward.

"I'd love to play hide and seek," said Sylvie, grinning. "And I've already met your friend. He showed me the way to your den." She pointed up into the sky, and Edward gasped. The star rabbit had gone back to where he came from. The shape of a giant rabbit was shining in the sky.

Edward lay down on the grass and Sylvie hopped over and lay next to him. He told Sylvie all about his games and adventures with the star rabbit. And as he looked up into the night sky, he thought he saw the star rabbit's eyes give a mischievous twinkle.

"I hope you'll stay," said Edward. "Now I know how much fun it is to have a friend to play with."

Sylvie nodded. "I've been looking for a friend too," she said. "I'd love to stay."

And as the sun rose and the stars disappeared, Edward and his new friend, Sylvie, fell fast asleep, hand in hand.

135

Shy Octopus

Harry was a shy octopus who lived in a quiet corner of the coral reef. He rarely came out and if he bumped into anyone, he would squeeze himself into the nearest crack and hide because, being a rubbery octopus, he could squeeze himself into places that no one else could reach.

One day, Harry was hiding when he heard a shout.

"Help!" cried a tiny voice. "It's me, Crab! I've fallen down a crack and I can't get out."

Harry peered out of his hidey-hole and watched as the other sea creatures did their best to rescue their friend.

First Seahorse tried to squeeze into the crack … then Angelfish … and finally Eel. But it was no use. They were all far too big. Harry knew that he would have to help, so he coughed shyly.

"Allow me," he said. And much to everyone's surprise, he squeezed his rubbery body into the crack and used a long tentacle to pull the tiny crab free. Everyone cheered.

"My hero!" sighed the tiny crab, smiling at Harry.

Harry blushed but felt very pleased. Maybe making friends wasn't going to be so difficult after all.

The Lonely Monster

People came from all over the world to spot the gigantic Lake Coco Monster, but no one had ever seen it. Then one day, a boy named Frankie was sitting by the lake when he heard a splash. He stayed very still, and he saw the monster creep out of the water. "Wow!" said Frankie. "You're no bigger than a kitten!"

The monster jumped. "Oh, please don't tell anyone you've seen me," it begged, trembling. "They'll be disappointed and they'll stop visiting the lake. I'll be lonelier than ever."

But Frankie knew better. "They'll love you!" he said. He showed the little monster how to play catch, and hide-and-seek. He brought his friends to meet it too, and soon the whole town knew what a perfect little monster was living in the lake. It had more visitors than ever, and the little monster was never lonely again.

Muddypaws and the Birthday Party

Ben was just a smallish, normalish boy, but he was Muddypaws' best friend. They went out for the best splishy-splashy muddy walks together. They made new friends together of all sizes, colors, and smells. They did everything together. But one sunny morning, Muddypaws woke up to find everything had changed in his house.

There were lots of new things! He sniffed about excitedly. What was happening? Where was Ben? He scampered off to find him.

"Woof!" barked Muddypaws, dropping his favorite ball at Ben's feet. "Let's play!"

But Ben was busy playing with a strange shiny thing. And the strange shiny thing was getting bigger ... and bigger ... and bigger ...

Ben's new game looked like fun! Muddypaws pounced on the mountain of strange shiny things. BANG! Muddypaws jumped away as fast as he could.

He didn't like that game! But what was that delicious smell drifting over from the kitchen ...? His tail began to wag. It was sausages! Surely no one would mind ... if he just tried a little one? But someone did mind!

"Bad dog!" scolded Ben's mom, and shooed him outside.

Muddypaws' tail stopped wagging at once. Why didn't Ben want to play with him? Why was everything different today? Maybe Honey the cat would want to play.

"Woof!" barked Muddypaws. "Let's go and play!"

Honey turned up her nose. She had better things to do than play with a puppy—like rolling on the grass in the sunshine.

Then the gate squeaked open ... and the front yard was filled with stamping feet, new smells, and loud voices.

A crowd of children ran up the path into the house. Something interesting was certainly going on and Muddypaws was stuck in the yard with no one to play with. The flowers were boring. The grass was boring. Even the smells were boring. And Muddypaws was getting hungry.

He tried to find his bone ... but it had disappeared.

What was happening inside the house? Maybe he would just look through the window to see.

Muddypaws pushed his nose up against the glass. Ben and the other children were running around and laughing.

They looked like they were having a great time! Muddypaws wanted to join in more than anything in the whole world.

Then Ben's mom walked into the room carrying something that was twinkling brightly. It was the biggest, most delicious-looking cake Muddypaws had ever seen, and it was covered in little lights.

Muddypaws licked his lips and pressed his nose even harder against the window. Suddenly, the door opened. It was Ben.

"Mom says you can come in now!" cried Ben.

But all at once, Muddypaws didn't want to come inside.

He didn't like the big shiny things that went bang!

He didn't like it when Ben's mom shouted at him.

He wasn't sure about all the new children in his house. It was all so different from normal.

"I know what to do," Ben said.

Ben threw Muddypaws' ball high into the sky.

At once, Muddypaws forgot about the big shiny things …

He forgot about the new children …

He even forgot about Ben's mom shouting …

Ben wanted to play with him! Muddypaws jumped and barked for joy. He ran as fast as he could to fetch his ball, and brought it back to Ben.

Ben scooped Muddypaws into his arms and gave him a big hug.

"I'm so sorry, Muddypaws," he whispered. "You didn't know it was my birthday. But you do know you're my best friend, don't you? And best friends do everything together. Even sharing birthday treats!"

"Woof!" barked Muddypaws happily, licking his lips. "Sausages!"

The King's White Elephant

Once upon a time, there lived a kindhearted, magnificent white elephant. He dearly loved his old, blind mother and took great care of her. They lived in a cave beside a beautiful lake surrounded by lovely pink lotus flowers.

One day, a forester lost his way in the forest and was terrified to find himself alone in the thick woods. He began to weep and call for help. The elephant was in the forest gathering fruit for his mother, when he heard the distressed cries of the man. He showed him the way out of the forest. The forester thanked the elephant and happily went home.

After some days, the forester heard the news that King Brahmadutta's personal elephant had died. He was looking for a new elephant. The forester remembered the kind white elephant, and thought that if he told the king about him, he would certainly get a reward.

The next day, the forester led the king to the white elephant's cave. The white elephant was upset at the forester's selfishness, but he didn't put up a fight because he didn't want to hurt anyone. He was led away to the king's palace. The elephant's poor mother guessed that the king must have taken away her son. She lay down in the cave and cried bitterly.

Meanwhile, the white elephant was given a grand reception in the royal elephant shed. The keepers laid out a feast for him, but he didn't touch the food. He just sat there with a sad expression on his face.

The king came to see what was wrong. The elephant told the king about his blind mother and how she couldn't survive on her own and would die.

The compassionate king was touched by the elephant's story and allowed him to return to his mother.

The white elephant took good care of his mother until the day she died. The king often used to visit him in the forest. And when the white elephant died himself, the king erected a statue of him by the side of the lake and held an annual elephant festival there in his memory.

The Vain Crow

Once upon a time, Crow was flying over the gardens of the King's palace, when he spotted a flock of royal peacocks proudly displaying their brightly colored tail feathers. He had never seen such beautiful feathers before, and he was filled with envy.

Crow's own feathers were dull and black. Every time he caught sight of his reflection, he felt unhappy.

"Oh, I wish I had shimmering feathers like the peacocks!" Crow sighed.

One day, Crow found several peacock feathers lying on the ground. They must have fallen from the peacocks' tails. Quickly, he collected them all and stuck them to his own black tail.

"Look at me!" Crow cried proudly, as he strutted up and down in front of the other crows. But the other crows just laughed at him and told him he looked funny.

"I'm going to join the peacocks," Crow cried. "I'm sure they'll be impressed!"

But when the peacocks saw Crow, they laughed too.

"You're not one of us!" they called. "Go away!" And they plucked out all the borrowed peacock feathers.

Poor Crow! Feeling very silly, he flew home. But when the other crows saw him, they scolded him and told him to go away.

Too late, Crow realized he should have been happy with who he was, rather than pretend to be something he wasn't.

Trixie the Troll

Long ago, after a wicked old troll had been caught bullying billy goats once too often, trolls from every corner of the globe were banished to a small land of gray skies and swirling mists at the bottom of the world.

At first, the trolls liked their new home. They were free to spend their days picking their enormous noses and making rude noises without the tiresome task of scaring humans and goats.

There was only one problem. Trolls had always lived alone under bridges and in caves. Many of them had never even met another troll! But in their small land, where there was barely space to scratch, their odors mingled to make one unbearable STINK!

For the first time they noticed that their fur was caked in food, their claws were filthy, and their breath was eye-wateringly horrific.

One shy little troll, called Trixie, felt so ashamed of her smell, she summoned all her courage and spoke up.

"Perhaps we should wash," she murmered.

The other trolls looked at her in disbelief. But Trixie was determined. She walked down to the river and gingerly dipped a slimy toe in the river, then waded in up to her knees and finally plunged into the current. It felt wonderfully cool and refreshing! As she laughed and splashed and a scrubbed, a few curious trolls gathered on the riverbank to watch. Before long they were all wallowing in the water, and by the time they had finished they smelt as fresh as mountain dew!

That was the start of a new way of living.

Now trolls are a clean bunch. They spend their days washing in the river, combing their silky fur, brushing their pearly fangs and clipping their spotlessly clean claws. But they still enjoy some of their old pastimes, like making rude noises, shouting silly things out loudly, picking their enormous noses, and proudly flicking their boogers at their friends!

Jack's School Trip

Jack loved everything about space. He read every space book he could find. He even dreamed about space at night. When his school visited the space center, he was so excited that he didn't notice the rest of his class walking ahead. When he looked around, he was alone. Which way had they gone?

Jack walked on and came to an open door with a little window in the middle. He stepped inside, the door clanged shut, and then he heard a voice. "BLAST OFF!"

"Uh-oh!" said Jack. There was a roar and the ground shook. Then he was whooshing into the air, faster than he had ever traveled. Jack was in a rocket, heading straight into space!

Floating upside down, Jack peered out through the little window. He could see the moon, the green-and-blue Earth, and lots and lots of stars. Then he saw an alien spaceship! Purple aliens with three eyes and five arms waved to him. Then he floated into the control room and saw the astronaut.

"Excuse me," he began. "I got lost and ..." But the shocked astronaut fainted on the spot. Jack gulped and sat at the controls, trying to remember everything he had read about rockets. Then he pressed a large "home" button and crossed his fingers.

WHOOOSH! The rocket turned and hurtled back toward Earth. It separated into three pieces and then a button for the parachute started to flash. Jack pressed it. A few seconds later he floated safely back to the space center. His class and his teacher were waiting for him. When the door opened, everyone started to clap! "This is the best school trip EVER!" said Jack.

Jack and the Beanstalk

There was once a young boy named Jack, who lived with his mother. They had no money and nothing left to eat.

"We have no choice but to sell Bluebell, our old cow," said Jack's mother. "Take her to market and sell her for a good price."

So Jack set off with Bluebell.

Before long, he met an old man, who asked, "Are you selling that fine cow?"

"Yes," Jack replied.

"Well, I'll give you these magic beans for her," said the man. "They don't look much, but if you plant them, you will soon be rich!"

Jack liked the sound of that, and he gave Bluebell to the man.

When Jack showed his mother the beans, she was very angry.

"Silly boy! Go to your room," she cried, throwing the beans out of the window.

The next morning, when Jack woke up, his room was strangely dark. He looked out of his window and saw a plant so tall that he couldn't see the top of it.

"It must be a magic beanstalk!" he cried.

Jack started to climb. When he reached the top, he saw a giant house. Jack's tummy was rumbling with hunger, so he knocked on the enormous door and a giant woman answered.

"Please may I have some breakfast?" asked Jack.

"You'll BE breakfast if my husband sees you!" said the woman.

Jack begged and pleaded, and at last the giant's wife let him in. She gave him some bread and milk and hid him in a cupboard.

Soon Jack heard loud footsteps and felt the cupboard shake.

"Fee-fi-fo-fum! I smell the blood of an Englishman!" roared the giant.

"Don't be silly," the giant's wife said. "You smell the sausages I've cooked for your breakfast."

When the giant had finished eating, he counted the hundreds of huge gold coins in his treasure chest. But the counting soon sent him to sleep.

As quick as a flash, Jack grabbed the coins, ran out of the house, and climbed down the beanstalk.

His mother was so happy to see the gold. "Clever boy! We'll never be poor again," she laughed.

But soon Jack and his mother had spent all the money, so the boy climbed up the beanstalk again. He knocked on the huge door and begged the giant's wife to give him some food. At last she let him in.

After eating his breakfast, Jack hid in the cupboard just as the giant arrived home for lunch.

When he had finished eating, his wife brought him his pet hen.

"Lay!" he bellowed, and the hen laid a golden egg. It laid ten eggs before the giant started to snore. Jack couldn't believe his luck, so he picked up the hen and ran.

His mother beamed when she saw the hen lay a golden egg.

"We will never be hungry again," she said.

Even though Jack and his mother were rich, the boy decided to climb the beanstalk one more time.

Jack knew the giant's wife wouldn't be happy to see him, so he sneaked in when she wasn't looking and hid in the cupboard.

When the giant came home, his wife brought him his magic harp.

"Play!" he roared, and the harp played such sweet music the giant soon fell asleep.

Jack saw his chance and grabbed the harp. As he ran, the harp cried out, "Master! Help!"

The giant woke up and began to chase Jack down the beanstalk.

"Mother, fetch the ax!" Jack yelled as he reached the ground. He chopped at the beanstalk with all his might. CREAK! GROAN! The giant quickly climbed back to the top just before the beanstalk crashed to the ground.

When his mother heard the harp play, she laughed and hugged Jack tightly.

"My clever boy!" she said. And the two of them lived happily ever after.

Little Dragon's Wagon

Little Dragon was walking in the sunshine. Buzz! went the bees. Tweet! went the birds. Squeak! went the bush …

"What can that be?" wondered Little Dragon.

It was a toy wagon, with one broken wheel spinning.

"Stay there, I'll get help!" called Little Dragon. He soon came back with his friends, Prince Pip, Princess Pippa, and Baron Boris. They were carrying a piece of rope to rescue the wagon.

Everybody helped, and they soon pulled the squeaky little wagon out of the bushes and back up on to the road.

"It's kind of old and smelly," said Pippa. "Let's give it a bath."

They pulled the wagon to Little Dragon's cave and he gave it a wash. Pip straightened the wheels. Pippa painted it with yellow dots. Then, last of all, Boris squirted some oil on to its wheels.

"I wish I had a wagon like yours, Little Dragon!" said Pip.

"Oh, but it isn't mine," said Little Dragon sadly. "I just found it. Now that it's fixed, I'd better take it back again."

The mealtime trumpet sounded from the castle on the hill ... and Pip, Pippa, and Boris had to hurry home to eat. Little Dragon waved goodbye, then set off by himself to take the wagon back down the hill. But the little wagon's wheels dug into the ground and it squeaked even louder than before.

Little Dragon pulled ... and pulled ... but it was hard work! So he sat down on the wagon for a rest. Suddenly the wagon started to roll down the hill! Faster and faster it went, steering around the curves as if by magic!

At last it stopped by the bush where Little Dragon had found it.

Little Dragon waved goodbye and started to walk back up the hill. He hadn't gone far when he heard a squeak. The wagon was right behind him!

"Would you like to come home with me?" asked Little Dragon.

"Squeak!" went the wagon, which meant, "Yes, please!"

So the magic wagon gave him a ride all the way back home.

Love Is Really Big

Willaby Wombat looked at his new baby sister snuggling in Mommy's arms. He had a funny feeling in his tummy that he couldn't explain.

"Mommy, do you love Winnie?" Willaby asked.

"Of course I do. I love her from the top of her fluffy little head all the way down to her teeny, tiny toes," replied Mommy. "Her smile makes me feel warm inside."

Willaby didn't feel warm inside. He just had that funny feeling in his tummy.

"Mommy, do you still love me?" he cried.

"Oh, Willaby! Of course I do. You're my special big boy," exclaimed Mommy.

"But Mommy," replied Willaby. "How do you know if someone loves you?"

Mommy put Winnie down in her little bed. "Come here, Willaby," she said, throwing her arms wide open. Willaby snuggled into Mommy's arms. His tummy still felt funny, but he did feel cozy and safe cuddled up to Mommy.

Mommy squeezed Willaby tight. "This is one way of showing someone you love them very much," she whispered in his ear.

Willaby snuggled in closer to Mommy. Mommy kissed Willaby on his cheek. "This is another way of showing someone you love them," added Mommy, softly.

Willaby grinned. "What does love feel like?" asked Willaby. "Does it make your tummy funny?"

"Love can feel like all sorts of things," explained Mommy. "It makes you feel special. It makes you feel happy. It makes you want to smile. It can make you want to jump for joy! Or curl up warm and snug. Sometimes, love makes your tummy feel like there are lots of butterflies fluttering around inside it."

Willaby squeezed Mommy closer. "But Mommy, does love make you feel like there are lots of kangaroos jumping up and down in your tummy?"

"Ah, my little Willaby!" Mommy sighed. "Is that what your tummy feels like right now?"

Willaby glanced over at his little sister. She was gurgling and giggling softly to herself.

"Yes. That's how my tummy feels, and it doesn't make me feel happy or special," he said.

Mommy picked up Willaby and swung him gently on to her back. She walked over to Winnie's little bed.

"Willaby, your tummy is telling you something else. I think you are feeling a little bit jealous of your new sister," she explained gently.

"What do you mean?" asked Willaby.

"Are you worried that because I love Winnie, I won't love you as much? Or have time for you?" asked Mommy.

Willaby nodded.

"It is normal to feel like that," Mommy added. "It will take you some time to get used to your new little sister."

Willaby snuggled closer into Mommy's back.

"But, Willaby, just because I love Winnie, it doesn't mean I don't love you." Mommy smiled. "There is plenty of room in my heart for both of you!"

Willaby climbed down off Mommy's back. The kangaroos in his tummy weren't jumping up and down so much any more.

"Can I hold Winnie?" he asked.

"Of course you can," said Mommy.

Winnie smiled up at Willaby. He began to feel all warm and fuzzy inside.

"Mommy," cried Willaby. "Love is really BIG, isn't it?"

"Yes, my darling!" Mommy laughed. "Love is everywhere and there is space for everyone."

"I love you, Willaby Wombat," Mommy said as she hugged Willaby close to her.

"I love you, too, Mommy," said Willaby.

"And you, Winnie," he whispered softly to his new little sister.

The Princes and the Water Sprite

Once upon a time there lived a king who had three sons. They were known as the Star Prince, the Moon Prince, and the Sun Prince. The king had his first two sons from his first wife, and his third son from his second wife. When his third son was born, he promised to give the second queen any gift she wanted.

Many years later when the three princes were grown up, the second queen asked the king for her gift. She wanted him to hand over the kingdom to her son.

"I can't do that, my dear," cried the king. "It is the custom for the kingdom to go to the eldest son. Please ask for something else."

The queen was cross and the king worried that she might try to harm the elder princes. So, with a heavy heart he sent them off to live in the forest, until they could come back and rule the city.

The youngest son decided to leave with his brothers. Soon they came to a pond. The pond belonged to a water sprite. He had the power to enslave anyone who came to drink from the pond and failed to give the correct answer to his question.

The Sun Prince went to fetch some water. When the sprite saw him, he asked, "What are the good fairies like?"

The Sun Prince replied, "They are like the sun and the moon."

"No!" shouted the sprite and he took the prince into his cave.

When he didn't return, the Moon Prince went to look for him.

"Oh, Prince, what are the good fairies like?" asked the sprite.

"They are like the sky above us," replied the Moon Prince.

"No!" screeched the sprite, and took him to his cave.

When the eldest brother came to look for his brothers, the sprite asked him the same question.

"If I get the answer right, you must return my brothers," demanded the Star Prince. "The good fairies are pure in heart and kindly in word and deed."

The sprite was so pleased with the prince's answer that he released his brothers from captivity.

The brothers lived happily together in the forest. When the queen died, they returned to the city, where the Star Prince became a wise and kind ruler.

The Bully and the Shrimp

Noah Shrimpton lived with his mom and his dad and his dog Dixie. He was small for his age, but he said being small was not so bad.

When Noah and his family moved house, Noah didn't like that very much. He missed his friends and he was a bit scared about starting at a new school.

On the first day, the principal Mrs. Johnson, took Noah to find his classroom. In the corridor, Noah bumped into a very tall boy.

"What's your name?" demanded the boy.

"Noah Shrimpton," said Noah with a big, friendly, I'm-new-but-nice-smile.

"SHRIMP-BOY!" jeered the boy.

Noah didn't know what to say.

"Connor!" said Mrs. Johnson. "We'll have none of that!"

Then she smiled at Noah. "Here we are. I'll introduce you to your teacher, Mr. Preston. I'm sure you'll like him."

"Good morning, everyone," said Mr. Preston. "We have a new boy in class today—Noah Shrimpton. Let's all say hello to him."

"Hello, Noah," the class said.

"Hello, Shrimp!" called out Connor.

"Connor, stop that!" said Mr. Preston. "Noah, come and sit over here with Ellie and Will."

Noah felt his face turning red like a tomato.

Everything was good the next day. To start with anyway. And then it happened.

Noah was having his juice when Connor bumped into him. Accidentally on purpose, Noah just knew it. Juice squirted all over his clothes.

Connor laughed and ran off grinning. Noah felt small and hot and ashamed.

"Are you okay?" asked Ellie.

"Yes," mumbled Noah. But he didn't feel okay.

After that, something bad happened every day.

Connor poured water over Noah's painting. He took Noah's bag and threw it around.

Wherever Noah went, whatever he did, there was Connor. Being mean.

It went on … and on … and on …

Once at recess, Ellie found Noah crying in a corner.

"Is it Connor?" she asked gently.

Noah nodded. Then he told her everything.

"Don't worry about him," Ellie said. "He's just one boy. I'm your friend. I like you."

Noah liked Ellie too. Just talking to her made him feel better.

But Noah didn't feel better for long.

The next morning, there was Connor in front of him. Big and mean.

"Stinky Shrimp!" yelled Connor. Noah was shaking, but he remembered what Ellie had said. And in a voice a bit like his own, but bigger, he shouted, "STOP! Don't call me Shrimp! It's not my name."

Connor looked surprised. He glared at Noah and ran off.

But that wasn't the end of Connor being mean. Or of Noah using his new, big voice.

A few days later, Connor pushed Noah. Hard. Noah fell backward on to the floor. He was scared, but he wasn't going to let Connor get away with it any more.

"STOP BULLYING ME!" yelled Noah, scrambling to his feet.

And Ellie was there, next to him.

"Go away, Connor," she said, "or we'll tell Mr. Preston."

All of a sudden, Connor wasn't so big and mean any more. He sort of shrank. And then he ran away.

Noah finally felt braver and stronger … he always knew being small wasn't so bad!

Noah really hoped Connor would leave him alone now, but when school finished, Connor walked up to Noah. Noah's heart thumped in his chest.

"I'm sorry," Connor whispered.

"What?" said Noah.

"I'm sorry, okay?" said Connor. "I won't do it again." And then he ran off.

Noah likes his new school now. And his friends Ellie and Will.

And Connor … well, he's not that bad either!

Super Robot

Tommy and Tristan were brothers. They both liked baseball (but they rooted for different teams), they both disliked broccoli, and they both loved robots. They tried to sneak broccoli on to each other's plates at supper. And they each wanted to win the Build A Robot competition.

Tommy and Tristan worked hard to make their robots and dreamed of beating each other. On the day of the competition, the organizer asked them what their robots did. "Mine's super strong," said Tristan. "It can lift anything!"

"Mine's super fast," said Tommy, pushing Tristan to one side. "It's quicker than a jet!"

Just then the organizer got a phone call. "Bad news," she said. "The judge's car has broken down miles away. I'll have to cancel the competition!"

Tristan and Tommy looked at each other. If they put their robots together, they could rescue the judge and save the competition. But could they forget their differences?

The brothers hammered, welded, and twiddled until they had built one giant super robot. Then they opened the control panel and tapped in their instructions. BEEP BEEP! The robot nodded and then ZOOM! It was gone!

The crowd held their breath as it sped out of sight. Could it rescue the judge? Then the robot reappeared, carrying the judge's car above its head. It put the car down and the judge stepped out.

"Who made this amazing robot?" he asked, smiling.

Tommy and Tristan stepped forward, arm in arm.

"I have already made my decision," said the judge. "You are the joint winners of the competition!"

Tommy and Tristan grinned at each other. Winning was wonderful, but the best part was working as a team!

The Tortoise that Couldn't Stop Talking

Tortoise lived by a little pond at the edge of the woods. One day when he was out walking, he saw two young geese swoop down on to the pond. Tortoise loved to talk, so he went over to chat to the geese.

"It must be wonderful being able to fly so high in the sky," he said. "I would love to be able to fly. I can only walk slowly!"

"Oh, it is wonderful," replied the geese. "We live in a beautiful home far away. We're going to fly back there tomorrow. Why don't you come with us?"

"How can I?" said Tortoise in surprise. "I don't have wings!"

"Don't worry, we can take you with us," said one of the geese. "But you must keep quiet the whole journey and not say a word to anyone."

Tortoise was very excited. "I can do that!" he cried.

The next day, the geese came to collect him. They were holding a long stick between them.

"Hold on to the stick with your mouth, and don't say a word until we reach home."

Tortoise grabbed the stick in his mouth and the geese flew up into the air. As they flew over a village, people started pointing and smiling at the sight of Tortoise dangling from the stick.

Tortoise looked down. The chatty fellow could not resist shouting out, "Look at me! I'm flying …"

But as he opened his mouth to talk, he lost his grip on the stick and fell to the ground with a huge CRASH!

Luckily, Tortoise landed in a grassy meadow. Apart from his injured pride, Tortoise was fine. But he had learned two valuable lessons: tortoises were definitely not born to fly and sometimes it is better to keep quiet!

The Three Little Men

There was once a girl named Helena who lived with her father, stepmother, and stepsister, Demona. Helena was kind and beautiful, but Demona was unpleasant and ugly.

The stepmother was an evil woman and vowed to get rid of Helena. "Go and gather strawberries, and don't come back without them," she told Helena one cold day.

The evil stepmother sent Helena out wearing only a paper dress and with just one crust of bread. Helena searched for many hours, but it was far too cold for strawberries to grow.

After a while she came to a little cottage. Feeling very cold, she knocked on the door. Three little men lived there and they let her in to sit by the fire.

"Why are you out in the cold wearing only a paper dress?" asked the men.

"My stepmother made me wear it. She has sent me to find wild strawberries," replied Helena.

Helena shared her small crust of bread with the three little men, although it was all she had. The three little men asked Helena to sweep the leaves from their path.

As Helena swept, the three little men decided to give her magic gifts, to reward her for her help.

"She shall become more beautiful every day," said the first little man.

"When she speaks, gold coins will fall from her mouth," said the second little man.

"She will marry a king," said the third little man.

As Helena swept the path, she noticed some wild strawberries. She filled her basket and returned home.

When the stepmother saw Helena's good fortune, she sent Demona to the cottage. But instead of a paper dress, she wore a fur coat. And instead of bread, she took a fine lunch.

Once at the cottage, Demona sat by the fire, eating her fine lunch, without sharing it. When the three little men asked Demona to sweep their path, she refused.

When the rude girl had left them, the three little men decided to give Demona some magic gifts.

"She shall become more ugly every day," said the first little man.

"Each time she speaks, a toad will jump from her mouth," said the second little man.

"She will live an unhappy life," said the third little man.

The magic gifts all came true. Helena married a king and lived happily ever after. Demona did not.

The Ox Who Envied the Pig

Big Red and Little Red were two large, strong oxen. They worked on a farm. All day long, they pulled the farmer's plow through the fields or heaved his heavy cart to market. By nightfall, they were exhausted, and fell into a deep, dreamless sleep in the farmer's barn.

On the farm, there also lived a little pig. The pig lived in the barn with the oxen, but while Big Red and Little Red were out working hard under the burning sun, the pig stayed by his sty, rolling in the mud and eating his food.

"Oh, look at him!" scoffed Little Red. "It's not fair. He should be working in the fields like us."

"At least we get to go and feel the wind and the sun, and hear the birds singing in the trees," said Big Red.

Meanwhile, the farmer was planning a big wedding for his daughter. He ordered his farmhands to start fattening up the little pig for the wedding feast.

One day, Little Red noticed that not only did the little pig do nothing all day, but now he was also being fed a rich and tasty diet.

"Brother, just look at the good fortune of this lazy little pig," he cried. "He does nothing all day and yet he gets to eat the most delicious food. It's not fair! We work hard all day and only get straw and grass to eat."

Big Red, who was the wiser of the two oxen, turned to his brother.

"Dear brother," he said. "Do not envy that poor beast. The farmer is fattening him up so he can be served for his daughter's wedding feast."

Little Red felt a bit foolish for envying such a terrible fate.

"It's better to eat dry straw and grass and live a long life," said Big Red wisely, "than to have a rich, tasty diet and end up on the farmer's table!"

From that moment on, Little Red stopped moaning about work, and started to enjoy his outdoor life.

Lazy Jack

Once upon a time there was a boy named Jack. He lived with his mother in a small cottage. They were very poor. The mother earned a few pennies by spinning, but Jack was so lazy he did nothing at all to help. Eventually Jack's mother told him that if he did not begin to work for his porridge, she would kick him out of the house and he would have to earn his living as best as he could.

Jack didn't want to leave home, so he went out and found a job for the day on a farm. The farmer gave him a jar of milk for his day's work. Jack took the jar and put it into the large pocket of his jacket. By the time he got home he had spilled it all.

"You silly boy!" cried his mother. "You should have carried it on your head."

"Next time I will," replied Jack.

The next day Jack found a job with a baker, who would give him nothing for his work but a large tom-cat. Jack took the cat and put it on his head, but in a short time the cat scratched him so much he was forced to let it go.

"You silly boy!" shouted his mother. "You should have tied it with a string and dragged it along after you."

"Next time I will," replied Jack.

The following day Jack hired himself to a butcher. The butcher gave him a large shoulder of lamb for his labor. Jack took the meat, tied it to a string, and trailed it along after him in the dirt. By the time he got home the meat was completely spoiled.

"Silly boy!" raged his mother. "You should have carried it on your shoulder."

"Next time I will," replied Jack.

Jack's next job was with a cattle keeper, who gave him a donkey for his trouble. Jack was a strong lad, but he found it difficult to hoist the donkey on his shoulder. At last he managed and started to stagger home slowly.

Now it happened that in a house on his route home, there lived a rich man with his only daughter, a beautiful girl, who had never spoken. The doctors said she would never recover her voice until somebody made her laugh. Her father had promised her in marriage to the first man who made her laugh.

As Jack staggered past the house, the girl happened to be looking out of the window. The sight of the donkey with its legs in the air was so comical and strange, that the girl burst out laughing and immediately recovered her voice. Her father was overjoyed and asked Jack to marry his daughter.

Jack and his mother were never poor again. They lived in a large house with Jack's wife and her father, happily ever after.

Dick Whittington and His Cat

Once upon a time there was a poor orphan boy named Dick Whittington, who lived in a little village in the countryside. He was often very hungry. He had heard tales about a faraway place called London, where everyone was rich and the streets were paved with gold, so he decided to set off for this wonderful place.

But when he arrived in London, there was no gold to be seen anywhere.

Disappointed and hungry, poor Dick slumped on to the steps of a rich merchant's house. The mean cook who worked there tried to shoo him away, but the merchant was a kind man and he took pity on Dick and gave him a job working in the kitchen. Even though the cook was mean to him, and he had to sleep in a small room full of rats and mice, Dick was very grateful to the kind merchant.

Dick saved up all his pennies and bought a cat to kill the rats and mice. After this, his life was much easier and he could sleep at night.

One day, the merchant, who was setting off on a voyage to the other side of the world, asked his household if anyone had anything they wanted him to take on his ship so that he could sell it for them. The only thing Dick had was his cat, so he asked him to take it.

"I will see what I can get for it," said the merchant.

And the kind merchant was true to his word. He sold Dick's cat to a king and queen who had a terrible rat problem in their palace. They gave him a ship full of gold, which the merchant passed on to Dick.

Dick was never hungry or poor again. He used his money wisely. He never forgot his kind friend the merchant, and when he grew up he married the merchant's daughter, and they all lived happily ever after.

The Crow and the Pitcher

One hot summer day, when there had been no rain for months and all the ponds and rivers had dried up, a thirsty crow was searching for a drink. At last he spotted a pitcher of cool water in a garden, and flew down to take a drink. But when he put his head into the neck of the pitcher, it was only half full, and the crow could not reach the water.

Now, the crow was a smart bird, so he came up with a plan—he would break the neck of the pitcher, then reach down to the water below.

Tap! Tap! Tap! The crow pecked the pitcher with his sharp beak again and again, but it was so hard and strong, he couldn't make even the tiniest crack.

The crow did not give up easily, so he thought of another plan. He would tip the pitcher over. The bird pushed and pushed as hard as he could, but the pitcher was very heavy, and it would not move at all.

The poor crow knew that if he did not get a drink soon he would die of thirst. He had to find some way of getting to the water in the pitcher! As he looked around, wondering what to do, he saw some pebbles on the path, and he had an idea.

He picked up a pebble in his beak and dropped it into the pitcher. The water level rose a little. The bird got another pebble and dropped it in. The water rose a little more. The crow worked very hard, dropping more and more pebbles into the pitcher until the water was almost at the top.

At last the bird was able to reach the water—and he drank and drank until he could drink no more. His clever idea had saved his life.

And the moral of the story is: little by little does the trick.

The Swineherd

Not all princes live in gleaming palaces. Some have modest kingdoms, few treasures, and only a crumbling castle to call their home. Once upon a time there was just such a prince. He was kind, smart, and handsome, and despite his noble birth, he had always been poor.

Soon the time came when the prince felt he was ready to marry. He didn't have great riches to offer a princess, but he was very well liked and young ladies lined up to accept his hand in marriage. But the prince had set his sights on the emperor's daughter. She was said to be beautiful and refined.

The prince decided to send the princess some gifts to prove his love for her. He chose the most precious things that he had: a beautiful rose from the tree that grew over his father's grave, and a divine song from his friend, a tiny nightingale, who lived in the castle garden.

The prince didn't know that the emperor's daughter was actually a spoiled and ungrateful girl. When she received the gifts, she threw the rose to the ground in a temper because it wasn't made of gold, and she sent the nightingale away when she saw that it was a dull brown color and not a jewel-encrusted clockwork bird.

But the prince was not ready to give up yet. He thought that if he was able to meet the princess in person, he could win her heart. Disguised as a poor farmhand, the prince went to the palace to ask for a job so that he might bump into her. The emperor needed someone to look after his pigs, so the prince accepted the job as his swineherd.

The prince had brought with him a special silver kettle, which had tiny bells on it. When the kettle boiled, the bells played a wonderful melody. He was boiling this kettle one day when the princess and her ladies-in-waiting came over to his shed by the pigsties.

"This music is divine. I must have that kettle!" she cried rudely. "How much will you take for it?"

"It will cost you one hundred kisses," said the prince.

The princess looked at him in disgust. He was covered in mud and smelled bad, but she desperately wanted the kettle, so she agreed. She was just about to deliver the last kiss when her father suddenly appeared.

"What a disgrace!" he shouted, and threw them both out of the palace gates.

Outside, the prince revealed who he really was. The princess dropped down into a curtsey.

"Oh poor me! Your Highness, what shall I do?"

"You mocked my gifts from the heart, but you would kiss a swineherd for the sake of a kettle!" said the prince. "Take it. I will have nothing more to do with you."

The prince set off home. The princess gazed
sadly after him. She was no longer wealthy, and all
she had now was a musical kettle!

The Sun and the Moon

In a village far away, there lived four brothers and a sister. The three older boys spent their time hunting for food for the family. But the youngest brother didn't do anything. He just stayed home with his sister, who cooked for him.

One day, the youngest brother and the sister had an argument.

"You are so lazy!" she cried. "I'm not going to make your dinner tonight." Then she stormed out of the house.

Outside, she saw a tall ladder leading up into the sky. She climbed it to see what might be at the top.

She was halfway up when the youngest brother came out of the house to look for her.

"Come back!" he called. Then he climbed up the ladder too.

Suddenly, when the sister got to the top, she
floated away and disappeared. Shortly afterward,
the same thing happened to her brother. The girl
became the sun and the boy, the moon.

Ever since then, the moon has been chasing the sun.
When the sun sets in the west, the moon rises in the east.

Every month, the moon fades away from hunger. Then, once
a month, the sun reaches out in pity and feeds the moon. He
grows full and happy again, but soon fades away without the sun.

This cycle happens every month and is known as the
waxing and the waning of the moon.

Sleepysaurus

Mommysaurus smiled at her son and cuddled him close. Sleepysaurus's eyes were starting to droop.

"Come on, sleepyhead!" she laughed. "It's time for bed."

But Sleepysaurus didn't want to go to bed.

"Bed's boring! I don't want to go to sleep. Sleep's boring! I want to read another story!"

"You're yawning," Mommysaurus said, gently tucking him bed. "That shows how tired you are."

"Yawns are boring!"

Sleepysaurus's mouth opened wider ... and wider ... but, just in time, he turned it into a ...

ROAR!

"What's all this noise?" said Daddysaurus, rushing in.

"It's Sleepysaurus," said Mommysaurus. "He won't go to sleep. He won't even let himself yawn!"

Daddysaurus smiled and read Sleepysaurus another story. And another ... and another ... and another!

Sleepysaurus felt an even bigger yawn coming on. His mouth opened wider and wider, but ...

ROAR!

"I have an idea, Sleepysaurus! Let's go for a walk. Maybe that'll tire you out," said Daddysaurus.

"Look at the beautiful stars," Daddysaurus said, when they stepped outside their cave. "Why don't you count them!"

"One, two, three, four, five …" counted Sleepysaurus. And by the time he'd gotten to fifty-six, he felt the most enormous yawn coming on.

His mouth opened wider and wider, but …

ROAR!

The sound echoed through the stillness of the night, getting louder and louder and louder …

But it wasn't an echo! It was a very big, very angry … T-Rex! And it was running toward them!

"Who's that waking me up?" roared the T-Rex.

Daddysaurus grabbed Sleepysaurus and raced, top speed, all the way home ...

"Roars are boring," said Sleepysaurus. "I think I'll go to bed now."

As Sleepysaurus climbed into bed he felt the most ginormous yawn coming on. His mouth opened wider and wider and ...

YAWN!

ZZZZzz!

Prudence Stays Up

Prudence the kitten was very excited. Mommy had promised to take her exploring by the light of the moon. "I can't wait! I can't wait!" meowed Prudence, running around in circles.

"You can only go if you have a nap this afternoon," warned Mommy Cat. "Otherwise you'll be too tired."

But Prudence was much too excited to take a nap. As soon as her mother had gone she padded around the farm to tell all her friends.

"I'm a big girl now!" she boasted. "I'll be out until dawn."

By dusk everyone knew about the exploring trip, but Prudence was nowhere to be found.

"Where can she be?" called Mommy Cat.

Suddenly she heard a loud snoring sound coming from high up in a tree. She looked up, and there was Prudence, fast asleep. All the excitement had worn her out. There would be no night exploring for Prudence tonight.

"Never mind," smiled Mommy Cat. "There's always tomorrow!"